Falling on Southport

by

M. J. Slater

Falling on Southport

Cover Art by *Teddi Black*

The Wild Rose Press, Inc.
PO Box 708
Adams Basin, NY 14410-0708
Visit us at www.thewildrosepress.com

Publishing History
First Edition, 2025
Trade Paperback ISBN 978-1-5092-6320-2
Digital ISBN 978-1-5092-6321-9

Published in the United States of America

Dedication

To Peggy, for all your support

Chapter 1

Sitting in the police station, my chest reverberated with the pounding of my heart. The interrogation room was dark and sterile, with a bright overhead light. I stared at my wedding ring, compulsively spinning it around my finger, begging it to release a clue, an answer to how I'd gotten here, accused of murdering my husband mere minutes after our marriage had imploded.

My mind was drawn back to our first meeting. A reporter on the college paper, I had arranged a meeting through a mutual friend to interview Vanderbilt's star point guard. Glancing up from my notebook, I caught sight of him, my mouth slightly ajar. Jim Hardy was a handsome man and clearly arrogant about his good looks the angle of his chin suggested. His hands were large, his mouth firm, and, as his eyes locked with mine, his lips turned upward, a delightful compromise between a leer and grin.

My eyebrows lifted along with the pen in my hand, an attempt at a neutral acknowledgement that he had found his target. His progression across the crowded coffee shop was slow, stealth and panther-like, garnering glances from the nearby co-eds. "I take it you're Abigail or maybe you're just another sorority girl in my gaggle of adoring fans."

"Gary said you could be a bit conceited." I tried to

get my voice under control. There was a slight quiver that the hiss of the latte machine hadn't covered up.

"Conceited or confident?" His grin widened. "Truly a fine line I thought I'd been managing with grace. Thank goodness you have been sent by the heavens to correct my mistake."

He was the requisite six feet, with blue eyes and a thick head of chestnut hair. I imagined quite a few ladies on campus had already run their hands through that hair.

"Well, thanks for meeting me. Gary said you were the star of the basketball team and who better to answer a myriad of basketball related questions. Sports isn't usually my beat. I got roped into writing this article," I babbled, cringing at my use of the word myriad and my apparent bookishness before this perfect specimen of a dumb hot jock, the likes of which had never looked my way before.

"Well, you'll be happy to know there are a *"myriad"* of reasons I agreed to this little interview." His eyebrows wiggled with glee as I involuntarily cringed. "Having never met the progeny of a well-connected political dynasty in person, I have been wanting to meet you, Abigail Lethican. Your grandfather is a great hero of mine, the longest serving senator from Illinois. You must be very proud of your father to pick up the baton."

"Well, he hasn't won yet. It's a very close race. Let's not jinx it." Though my smile was demure, my gut response was to be both flattered and alarmed. My family had been in politics for generations. On the North Shore of Chicago, everyone in our town had known my family's connection to politics. I'd been raised to smile politely and never make a scene. Arguments were for the dinner table, not to be witnessed by outsiders. It wasn't a bad way to grow up. It was a heady feeling to be so close to the engine of power and able to take such pride in my grandfather's good deeds, though I'd always felt my life was under a microscope. In Nashville, after three and a half years at Vanderbilt, the relative anonymity had been a glorious respite.

This had been my one chance to just be me, Abigail, from Chicago, with a major in business and minor in creative writing, not Senator Lethican's granddaughter. Jim's mention of my pedigree must have brought a modicum of surprise to my face (never shock—that expression had been bred out of the Lethican genes decades ago). "You're surprised I researched you." His grin was sheepish but still managed to take on a tone of condescension.

"As the interviewer, it comes as a bit of a surprise," I said, regaining my composure.

"Well, I just like to know a bit about the person who may potentially immortalize my spoken word."

"That seems a bit dramatic for a story on basketball, no?"

"Perhaps, but, I have to be honest with you. I'm more than just a pretty face." His eyelashes fluttered theatrically, absurd but sweet. The requisite giggle bubbled from my mouth.

"A political career has been a dream of mine. I'm actually pre-law and poly sci and am taking the LSAT next week."

"Well, I'm impressed, Jim Hardy. Where do you find the time to get your studying done with all the hours a star basketball player needs to spend in the gym?"

"I'm a man of many parts," he replied. His broad chest leaned forward, caging the small coffee table with his arms, creating a sense of intimacy. "Seriously, I would love to pick your brain about politics if you have time later…not to put any conditions on this interview, but it would mean a lot to me."

His roguish smile, the leer gone, seemed constructed just for me. My breath caught. "Of course, Jim, everyone knows in politics it's a lot of tit for tat."

We met again later in the week in a study room in the library. After two hours rehashing my grandfather's senate campaigns, Jim stood up, stretching his arms overhead. "I'm starving, Abigail. Is there any chance I could take you to dinner?"

I might not be the prettiest girl, but my figure was good, slim and athletic. Behind my thick glasses were pale blue eyes. A short blond bob my mother called sophisticated was meant to steer you away from my pronounced chin. There was no reason this demi-god couldn't be interested in me. It just seemed unlikely when compared with the usual southern girls, their hair sausage curled, lash extensions seemingly fixed on before sunrise. Maybe I was a welcomed break from the legions of vacuous cheerleaders at his beck and call. It must have been a relief to him to have found someone as interested in politics as he was.

I agreed to dinner and never looked back. The first time we went to a party, it was impossible to ignore the whispers of, "I can't believe he'd pick her."

It didn't matter. When we were alone, he truly seemed to enjoy my company. What we had was real.

There was so much to talk about.

One night in that first week, after many bottles of wine, he reached across the couch and cradled my face in his large hand. My breathing quickened as my cheek nuzzled his calloused hand.

"Abigail, you have the bluest eyes." His face inched closer and his lips grazed my temples.

"I didn't know you were such a student of eye color or I certainly would have mentioned it."

"Always quick with the joke. If you don't want me to kiss you, just say so." His breathing was still deep as his hand stroked the back of my head, but his eyes looked into mine with a hardness about them. A moment of irrational fear gripped me. He was a man who was going to get his way. His mission to make love to me was born of determination, not an outpouring of passion.

My eyes closed and my body leaned in for a kiss, refusing to let my mind ruin this moment. I wanted Jim to pick me, to be the one he desired. Shaking off my doubts, one arm reached across his muscular shoulders while the other one tangled in his luxuriously thick hair.

As our kiss grew deeper, tongues flicking, exploring, his hand reached up under my thin t-shirt. "It's a mighty warm evening, Miss Abigail." His grin caused an electrical reaction in my body. "Can I help you with this shirt?"

"Oh yes, that would be nice," I managed to reply. My shirt was off and a second later, his kisses covered my collarbone, tracing the outline of my bra strap with his fingers.

"Miss Abigail, you'd be much more comfortable without this contraption."

There was no inexpert fumbling of a 21-year-old male trying to undo a bra strap. In seconds, it was off with ease.

He arched an eyebrow at my bared chest. "I do declare, Miss Abigail, I think you wear that pushup bra just to fool the boys." He began to graze my nipples with his lips and for that I was grateful. I could not have hidden the hurt in my eyes. My few experiences had been with men who had expressed utter gratitude at the chance to spend an amorous interlude with me. My breasts were flat, it was true, but not as flat as he had made me feel in that moment. Jim worked his way down, pulling my skirt and panties off with a yank.

After a few cursory explorations with his tongue on my most delicate of female parts, he unceremoniously pulled his pants down, reaching for a condom in his pocket. "Well, thank you for that, at least." My expression must have been one of disbelief.

"Cute." He grabbed my hips and gave himself to me with a vigorous thrust. "Are you saying you would have refused me, Abby?" His body pushed against mine. "I can't see that happening."

Afterwards, spent, he looked at me with his old softness from before. "I'm starved. Let's grab a sandwich, yeah?"

The next few days had me thinking about our lovemaking. It had not been good, but perhaps that was my fault. Beauty was just as much about attitude as it was about looks.

I went shopping for sexy lingerie, convinced that it would make all the difference. The next evening, when he began kissing me with that same determination, I spoke up. "Hold on a minute, would you? I have a surprise."

Donning my new attire, I stepped out of the bathroom, doing my best to channel my inner sex kitten.

"Oh, Abs, some women can pull off lingerie, and some can't. Let's not try anymore, okay?" Jim stripped me down and continued on with his efficient lovemaking.

****

"Weren't you the one who said, the hotter the guy, the worse he is in bed?" I asked my friend Lucy. She looked at me, perplexed.

"Yes, but I meant they were hurried and rushed and self-absorbed, not militant in finishing. This guy sounds like a terrible lover, Abby. Are you even attracted to him? Maybe he thinks you're not turned on?"

"Oh, come on, you've seen him. My eighty-year-old grandmother would yearn for him." I frowned, embarrassed.

"Ha. Gross. Besides a mild flutter in my nether regions, he doesn't do it for me. He seems like one of these guys that only thinks of his own finish."

"God, this is too much. Forget it."

"Seriously, Abby, how do you feel the rest of the time you're with him?"

"Good, great. We make a great pair. He's smart, ambitious, we both love politics. It feels good to be with someone who is interested in me for my mind, actually." My voice was weak.

"Okay, Abby, I get it. He's quite the catch." Lucy abruptly switched topics, finished with my mediocre sex life. "So, did you hear about Denise Ryerson throwing a drink in Yvette's face last night?"

****

A few weeks passed, and Jim and I grew closer. When we were out together, he made me feel like a princess at a ball, putting his hand on the crook of my elbow and leading me around the room like a jewel to be displayed. "Abby here is one of the smartest gals you'll ever meet. She's political royalty. Knows all of Washington," he'd drawl, perfecting his good ole boy wink.

Our sex life improved with time, though it still felt like Jim thought sleeping with me was a chore. Would it be worth it to give up an otherwise perfect relationship for more of a spark? Unlikely. Too many single girlfriends were telling me how hard it was to meet anyone who could read and actually owned a toothbrush.

Alone, we would talk about his ambition to go to the University of Chicago for law school, become a partner in some top-notch firm and then launch his political career. Talking politics brought him to life like nothing else. Arguing politics late into the night was an aphrodisiac. This was our common ground. Picturing myself as part of a successful team building our future together anchored me in the relationship.

Growing up in a family like mine, it was hard not to want to be part of a political power couple. My grandfather consulted my grandmother in everything. She was the one who finessed his private life, made friends with the wives of important men, kept his appointment diary full, and matched his suits and ties in the morning. Theirs had been a partnership of equals, laced with tenderness.

When the guests had left after some fundraiser, he

would take her hand, kiss it gently and say, "Another success, don't you think, dear?"

Though that tenderness was lacking in my relationship with Jim, I could hone the same partnership. Perhaps being a constant object of desire had deflated his own desire. I'd been victim to many a rogue elbow standing next to him at a party, another woman with too much cleavage and day-glow teeth trying to get his attention. His flirtatious nature was polished, engaging but distant, with a hint of contained danger, like an object that could burn you if you got too close.

As the months went by, his story came out bit by bit. Born into a poor but proud Southern family, this confident athlete had been the popular small-town wonder, winning a basketball scholarship to a big name school. The pictures, stuck up around his small room with sticky tack, showed his parents smiling proudly at his graduation. One was a picture of him at prom, with his cousin, a stunning but petite woman, all curves and pouty lips. When asked why his cousin would be his prom date, the response reflected his protective nature. "How else was I to keep her from the wolves? You have to keep your family safe." His gaze remained fixed on the picture. "Lee is great. You'll meet her sometime. She's actually here in Nashville studying to be a paralegal."

"I look forward to meeting any of your family. It would be great to visit your parents. Sleeping on a blow-up bed or a couch or wherever is fine with me. What is important is meeting the people close to you."

"You'll meet them when they come up. If I brought you home, you'd just make them nervous. They

M. J. Slater

wouldn't know what to do around someone manor born, such as yourself."

"I am not manor born." My reply was tart. "That's absurd. I would never do anything to make them or anyone feel inferior. Where you come from matters to me…because I am starting to have serious feelings for you."

A nervous quiver took hold of my voice. There had been no declarations of love on either part. We were almost like good friends who occasionally had sex. Sure, he had introduced me as his girlfriend, but he was so hard to read, so poised, determined-determined in basketball, in school, even in social climbing. The insecurities and shame about his humble beginnings were palpable. That pained me but I understood wanting more, and God help me, that made me love him. My strength and connections were something no one else could give him and that gave me sustenance.

"Well, if you're not ready to introduce me to your family, what about coming home and meeting mine? Thanksgiving is always a bit of a crush of people but the food is good and my siblings are a lot of fun."

"All three of your older brothers in one room? Should I be scared?" His broad smile shifted the mood. While not ready to let me into his family, this man seemed excited to enter mine.

In the morning, I called my mother to tell her to expect another guest. "Abby, this is so exciting! You've never brought home a young man before. Is this serious? Is he the one? I'll tell your brothers to be on their best behavior."

"Thanks, Mom. I'm excited for you to meet him. He's really special to me. I think I love him."

10

Vulnerability and happiness intertwined around my heart. The words quietly tested themselves on my tongue.

The week before Thanksgiving, Jim seemed apprehensive about our upcoming trip. "Are you having second thoughts about meeting my family, Jim? I know it's a lot of people. If you're uncomfortable, we can stay here."

"No! I want to meet your family. I wouldn't miss this opportunity."

Registering the surprise on my face, he continued less forcefully, "It's an honor to meet your family. It's just that…."

"What is it?"

"Good table manners weren't part of my upbringing."

"I've eaten with you plenty." I laughed. "You have yet to pick your teeth with a fork."

"Well, obviously, I'm not a brute. It's just that with all the glasses and forks and spoons, I'm afraid I'll make a mistake." Blushing for the first time since we'd met, his embarrassment was palpable. It was clear how much of his demeanor had been carefully cultivated to be one of strength and bravado.

"That's nothing. My family won't judge you on which fork you use."

"People are always judging you, Abigail, whatever you tell yourself."

"Okay, okay, take it easy." I thought for a minute. "What if we do a few practice runs? We'll set up a place setting and you can practice."

"You're telling me you have all that glassware here in this tiny little studio apartment? Are you hiding it under the bed?"

"No, I'll just run over to Home Goods and buy a couple of things. You'll learn it all in no time."

The next day, he sat at my kitchen table looking perplexed. "All of this? I need all of this silverware?"

"It's easy. There's a pattern to it."

He took his napkin out and grumbled, "I feel like goddamn pretty woman."

A crooked smile signaled his confidence returning. I would do anything to make this man unstoppable. My heart thumped. It felt good to be needed.

"Let's begin," I said, picking up a fork.

****

A week later found us exiting the terminal at O'Hare. Stepping into the chilly air, I pulled my scarf tighter around my neck and reached for Jim's hand. We hadn't talked much on the flight, both busy editing papers—Jim with his noise canceling headphones, jaw clenched, a determined furrow on his brow. My approach was more lackadaisical—crunching on pretzels, twisting my hair absentmindedly and wondering if I should dye it some crazy color before my school days were behind me. I'd enjoyed my summer internship at Wasmussen Bank and was waiting for an offer. The people were smart, competitive but not killer. The CEO was also friends with my grandfather, so the offer was likely a done deal. Perhaps I should have tried harder to be my own person. Life seemed too confusing at 20. It had been easier to take the helping hand. I never felt stifled by my family. My brothers had felt the need to strike out on their own, to make their identity unique. I, on the other hand, had let privilege wash over me, wrapping me up safely and securely. I liked the order and ease of my life. A determined and solid man like Jim would protect me. It would be easy to stay safe in his shadow. My mother pulled up in her black SUV.

"A brand new Audi, Mom? Got tired of the Lexus?"

"Well, Tommy needed a car now that he's moving out to LA. It would be silly to get him a new car in such a busy city." She smiled sweetly. "Enough about the car, Abigail. Introduce me to this handsome man."

Jim reached out his hand.

"This is my mother, Alice."

"A pleasure, Alice."

"Well, hop in. You sit up front with me, Jim. We can get to know each other. I'm happy you decided to join us. You won't be bored, though you may not be able to get a word in edgewise. Traditionally, Wednesday is takeout of the Chinese variety. Afterwards, while I do prep for tomorrow, the children team up and make pies. It's quite a competition."

"Mom, I'm the youngest at twenty-one. Perhaps we could use a different word than 'children'?"

"Nonsense. You are, after all, my children. Now, Jim, you can team up with Abby and Will. Devin and Tommy tend to make a mess and have an inability to follow a recipe, and Abby says you are much more meticulous in your cooking."

I blushed a deep red in the backseat, grateful for the waning light. It was something mentioned to my mother in passing. We usually ate together at the dining hall, but when we did occasionally cook, Jim was precise in his measurements, each spill immediately cleaned, his need for control in any situation obvious.

13

Embarrassed that my mother had chosen to divulge this personal tidbit, I brushed it off flippantly. "I thought it wise to warn her you're a neat freak and her house would remain spic and span if she allowed me to bring you."

Glancing into the backseat, Jim's eyes looked at me warily. "Well, hopefully everything else you shared has been positive." The steel edge of his voice cut through the delicate notes of Chopin my mother had selected for our drive.

"Of course, Jim." My face remained impassive at his scolding tone.

"Well, I was thrilled to hear you were so neat. My husband is very organized as well. Organizational skills are a great indicator of your future success in life." With that, my mother, the intuitive politician's wife, eagerly embarked on the remaining weekend schedule. "Where was I…well, tomorrow is obviously Thanksgiving. Friday, we could go skating downtown and do a little gawking at the holiday decorations. Saturday, we are organizing a toy drive. We'd love your help, though it's your vacation if you'd prefer to just relax. Then Sunday you're leaving so early."

"Yes, we thought we'd miss the airport rush and take the first flight out." As we drove in the now dark streets of Winnetka, the stately Colonials and occasional Queen Annes, homes of a bygone era, were already outfitted with holiday lights.

"It looks like a Norman Rockwell scene. The perfect place to spend the holidays." His tone was appreciative.

"Yes, it is nice," my mother replied. "I love Thanksgiving especially. I love that it's about people and conversation. Christmas is nice, but there is so much pressure on gift giving. It's really more of a children's holiday, and until one of my four children gives me a grandchild, I guess I can't properly appreciate it."

"Well, maybe you should drop that hint to your oldest, not your youngest, Mom," I snipped.

We turned onto the small lane leading to our house. Beyond the next street, the swells of Lake Michigan rolled in a tumult. The car nosed its way down the hill.

"We're here," I said brightly, as we turned in the driveway.

"Wow, this is quite the house."

"It's one of S. S. Beman's Tudors. He didn't do very many houses up here. I think that makes it rather special. There's a touch of romance about a classic English style Tudor. You should see the garden in the summer. It really feels like you might be in England," my mother said. "I'm sure you'll be back sometime this summer, you're always welcome."

We grabbed our suitcases and opened the door to the mudroom. Our Great Dane loped through the door.

"Oh, wow, that is the largest dog I've ever seen."

"Yes, he's large, even for a Great Dane. Ridiculously, he is also named Dane. I'm not sure what we were thinking. Abby can take you upstairs. Her room is on the third floor, so it's quite a hike. Settle in and we'll see you in about an hour for dinner."

As we trudged up the stairs, Jim whispered, "Are we sleeping in the same room together? That doesn't seem appropriate."

"We are adults. If you're uncomfortable, you can sleep on the couch, but really, they don't mind. My mom turned the guest room into her office and my brothers are all probably staying here for the weekend."

Jim took a deep breath. "Okay. Most Southern mothers would not be so understanding."

"Is sharing a bed with me so terrible?" My hand brushed his broad back in a lingering caress.

"No, of course not, Abs. I look forward to being in close quarters with you." We reached the third floor. "Who else is up here with us?"

"Just us, the other room up here is the TV room."

"Your brothers are all downstairs?"

"Yes. Were you thinking of enjoying a little private time before dinner?" My palm lay flat on his muscular chest; my lips softened for a kiss.

Jim pulled back. "Really, Abby, I don't think that's appropriate."

Stepping away quickly, the magnitude of his disgust felt like an assault. "You're right. We would just be waiting for someone to walk in. I'm going to take a shower. Feel free to make room in the closet if you want to unpack." Quickly reaching for the robe draped on the chair, my legs carried me to the bathroom. The door safely locked behind me and I looked in the mirror. My strained face was pale and my hair slightly greasy after the flight. Was Jim to blame for finding me unattractive in such a state? Shaking off the feeling of rejection, I told myself he was just not a sexual person, and probably really nervous to meet my enormous family.

Since my departure, my parents had upgraded the bathroom. The multiple jet sprays hitting my body felt luxurious. Feeling rejuvenated, I stepped out gingerly and wrapped my angular body into my bathrobe. The steam was clinging to every surface in the room and it seemed best to leave the supercharged vent on. Padding back to my room, the door was open. Jim's massive body was hunched in the chair, speaking low into the phone. "You know I love you. Yes, of course I miss you."

I knocked softly, causing Jim's head to snap up, his face stiff with anger. "Listen, I have to go. I just wanted to wish you a happy Thanksgiving, Gram."

"I'm sorry. You didn't need to end your conversation because of me."

"It's fine. I just called to say hi and tell them I arrived. They are upset I didn't come home for the holiday," he said, not looking at me, bending down to plug his charger in. "You know, I'm just going to turn this thing off and enjoy my time here." His arms snaked around my waist, pulling me in. "You look very fetching in that bathrobe." His tongue nudged open my parted lips. The intensity of his passion left me quivering and confused. It was a kiss designed to distract me. We pulled apart as suddenly as we began. "We should be getting downstairs. Why don't I run down and let you dress?" Tucking in his shirt and running a hand through his hair, he turned and left the room.

The spontaneity of the kiss had left me off kilter. It saddened me he hadn't shared his family's disappointment that he had come north instead of going home for the holidays. It hadn't occurred to me to ask what they did for Thanksgiving. Once Jim agreed to come and meet my family, any concern for his family had slipped my mind. A note to his grandmother might go a long way in smoothing things over with them.

Downstairs, Jim was helping my mother unfold card tables. She glanced up as I entered the room. "I thought this year the kids would enjoy being on their own in the living room. They are old enough, I think, and this way I won't get a dirty look from Lisa every time a political topic not appropriate for little ears comes up…" My mother rolled her eyes. My parents had raised us differently, talking about anything and everything, voicing their opinions and asking us about ours.

"Well, you've always been very open with us, maybe to a fault. She's just not comfortable with that. It's her choice, her kids, Mom." I looked at Jim. "Lisa is my mother's niece. She has four kids and they live a few blocks away. They always come for the holidays."

"My sister died of breast cancer when Lisa was twelve. I've tried to be more than just an aunt to her. It's such a hard age to lose a mother, and Lisa was always such a sensitive girl." She paused. "Well, it's always hard to lose your mother. Mine is still alive and most of the time she doesn't know me anymore. She has Alzheimer's, but I can't bear the thought of her passing."

"Lisa is like a sister to me," I added.

Jim looked down, his face serious. "You know my mother passed away from breast cancer the summer before college. I was always glad she got to see me graduate high school, but I miss her every day."

I froze, not allowing the surprise to register on my face. Jim had never mentioned his mother's death to me, let alone said anything about her suffering from cancer. When asked about the pictures in his room, he had pointed out his mom and dad at his high school graduation with no mention of her passing. Had he intentionally kept it a secret or was the memory just too painful? I fought the urge to wrap my arms around him. The mudroom door slammed shut in the kitchen, followed by my father's trademark whistle.

"Dad?"

"There's my little girl." My tall and lanky father swept into the room, his coke-bottle glasses fogging up. His arms wrapped around me, still cold from the outdoors. "I've missed you, Nightingale."

"Nightingale?" Jim asked.

"Dad called me 'Abigail-Nightingale' as a child. He's an avid bird watcher."

"I do my best thinking on an early morning walk with a pair of binoculars. You must be Jim." My dad reached out his hand.

"Senator, it's a pleasure and an honor to meet you. I followed your race very closely. I thought your opponent used some dirty tactics. That attack—"

"Oh well, it's in the past," my dad said. "Please call me John. We're so pleased Abigail has brought you home for Thanksgiving. Now, if you'll excuse me, I'm going to put on some dry clothes." Heading toward the stairs, he paused to kiss my mother's cheek.

Jim looked discomfited. It was clear he'd been practicing his introduction to my father and appeared disappointed it had been cut short. A surge of protective love swelled within me. His vulnerability made me feel protective.

Jim's jaw was tight as he turned toward my mother. "What's next, Alice?"

"If you go down those stairs to the basement, there will be some folding chairs in the first room on your left."

When Jim had disappeared down the stairs, my mother whispered, "He seems nice, though quite serious. Why didn't you tell me about his mother?"

Trying not to blurt out the truth, my reply was weak. "It seemed personal and I didn't know if he wanted me to." Before my mother could ask her next question, Jim came into the room carrying several folding chairs laced up his arms.

"Thank you so much, Jim. That would have taken me several trips. My, you must be strong." I rolled my eyes at her. "Abigail, why don't you take the car and pick up the food. It should be ready soon. The keys are in my purse."

We walked to the mudroom and pulled on our winter boots and coats. "Looks like it's really starting to come down," I said. "The embarrassing truth is I fulfill every stereotype of a suburban female driver. Would you mind driving?"

"I don't mind, but are you sure your mom is okay with that?"

"Her mom will thank you for keeping the residents of Winnetka safe!" my mother yelled on her way to the kitchen.

Jim smiled. "Okay, let's go." Pulling out of the driveway, Jim looked around the interior, taking in the plush leather seats and wood paneling. "This is definitely the nicest car I've ever been in. You know, a guy could get used to this."

"Ha, well, a girl could get used to being chauffeured around."

"If you're so opposed to driving, when we settle down, it will have to be in the city, somewhere near a train line."

"Maybe two train lines, just to be safe." As we drove slowly down the slippery side streets, the snow heavy and thick, my heart fluttered. "So you think we have long-term potential?" I ventured.

"Yeah, don't you? You're not really the type of girl a guy picks for a fling."

The backhanded compliment was a clear reference to my lack of pin-up girl looks. "Are you attracted to me?" I spoke into the soft darkness.

The quiet in the car was deafening. Jim took a deep breath. "I'm attracted to your mind, Abs. You're so smart and accomplished and so different from other girls. You're someone I can see by my side as I build a career. You're a perfect partner and there is beauty in that."

Clenching my hands, my fingernails biting into my skin, I wondered how to respond. A declaration of explosive desire toward me would have been false. His own good looks took center stage in my mind as I thought about the reverse scenario. Would my attraction to him be as strong if he wasn't movie star material? The answer was yes. I enjoyed talking to him, seeing his brain pick apart intricate problems. His confidence was like a beacon—though it was true that came part and parcel with his looks. The fact was, I never wanted to go let go of this man. Anyway, wasn't it better to be loved for my true self, not treated as a trophy?

My response came out slowly. "I think we are on the same page. We fit together in our own unique way. We could be great together and build a life with real meaning."

The road grew more treacherous, requiring all of

Jim's concentration. We drove in silence, the GPS chirping out directions every few minutes.

Back from our errand, I saw my brothers had all arrived. "Hey! We brought dinner. You guys want to grab some bags?"

"Coming!" Tommy, the second youngest, came down the hallway. "Hey, I'm Tom. You must be Jim. Let me take that."

"Thanks. Nice to meet you. I'll go get the rest out of the car."

Tom and I took the bags to the kitchen while Jim went back outside. We took out the containers and began arranging them around the island. Tom gave me a big bear hug from behind. Leaning into his warm strength, I looked at my other brother, sitting at the counter scrolling through his phone without so much as a glance up. "Devin, so nice to see you after so long and, by the way, can you be bothered to stand up and maybe grab plates and silverware?"

Devin looked up. "You seem to have things well under control with your little minion there." Tom balled up a paper bag and threw it at Devin's head. There were always a lot of flying projectiles growing up with so many brothers.

"Come on, dude, get a move on," Tom said.

"Eloquent as always, Tom. Where's your new heartthrob, sis? I hear he's a dreamboat."

"Devin, would you just shut up and get the plates?" said Tommy in a faux stage whisper.

"I'm right here, ready to be observed. Please tell me if you see any flaws," Jim spoke just behind me.

I blushed all the way to my roots and turned around, reaching my hands out. "Let me take those bags. Please ignore Devin. He's my least favorite brother."

Devin and I had always had the most antagonistic relationship amongst the siblings. Will was the oldest, protector to all his little brothers and sister, but slightly aloof. Devin was born indignant, no doubt as a result of being second in line, and proceeded to live life with a chip on his shoulder. Tom, the third, was the kindest, always there with a helping hand. He was only eighteen months older than me. We had been the closest, best friends since we were little kids chasing each other around on big wheels down the driveway. I knew all my brothers would be there for me, but Tom was the one who understood my deepest insecurities and my wildest dreams. We texted almost daily. He had taken a job out in LA at a design firm and I was heartbroken he would be moving across the country soon, just as I was set to move back in a few months after graduation.

Jim went back to the car for the last of the bags. Once he was out of earshot, Devin drawled in his best southern accent, "He's way too good looking for you, honey child."

"Seriously, Devin, why do you always have to be such an ass? Maybe not all men are shallow like you."

"Or maybe it's your trust fund and your famous last name," Devin sneered, his lips curled into a smirk.

The tears rose unbidden in my eyes and I bit my lip to keep them at bay. "Not nice, Devin, though you really do have a way with words. Shocking it's taken you five years, completely financially dependent on our parents, to write your great American novel. How's that going, by the way?" Storming out, I made my way to the powder room.

Devin had always known how to push my buttons. He was like the evil voice in my head, the one that always denigrates your best intentions.

Splashing water on my face, I took a frank assessment of my looks. I was pretty enough, my face plain and almost birdlike. My eyes were a milky blue behind the thick tortoise shell glasses. It didn't matter. Jim's early declaration about our future gave me confidence. I squared my shoulders and promised myself I wouldn't make eye contact with Devin for the rest of the night. The banging on the door made me jump, knowing only Devin would be so rude. Ready to do battle, I opened the door.

"Sorry, I was waiting for you to apologize but you were taking forever." Devin scowled.

"Seriously, just leave me alone. Why am I the only one you pick on?"

"Well, obviously, you're an easy target." His teasing note only infuriated me more.

I shoved him hard. "I'm done. I have zero desire to talk to you the rest of the weekend. Enjoy your Thanksgiving."

He grabbed my arm. "Look, I know I'm your least favorite, but know that I'm trying to watch out for you in my own way. You are my family and no matter what you think, family means a lot to me."

Eyeing him warily, I wrenched my arm free. "Am I supposed to thank you for your insight? I'm a grown woman making grown up decisions. I don't need my big brothers telling me what is or is not wrong with my relationship. Not to mention, you've barely said two words to him. Maybe you're the one being shallow. It's just silly. I know our truth."

Devin looked down, his loose floppy blond hair over his eyes. "Sure, okay, you're both desperately in love and I'm just here to sneak some of Dad's good scotch when he isn't looking. Friends?" He stuck out his palm.

"Fine, friends," I said, extending my arm.

"Too slow." He smirked, raking his hand through his hair.

"You're such a child." I stormed off, heading back to the kitchen.

Tom and Jim were putting out the food on the counter and making small talk. "That was an amazing three pointer," Tom said. Evidently, as men do, they had found commonality in sports.

"Where's Will?" I interrupted. "Wasn't his car in the driveway?"

"He just stopped by to steal a bottle of wine before heading over to Carol's parents' house. They're having some guests over. He'll be by for pie making later."

"Well, he could have said hi."

"Don't pout, Nightingale. I think he wants to sneak in a few words with Carol's dad before the festivities start. I did a little snooping at his place last weekend and spied one doozy of ring in his bureau drawer."

"No way! It's about time." I looked at Jim. "He and Carol have been together for years. I don't know what took him so long."

"Is there a time limit to dating before a proposal has to happen?" The arch expression in his eyes made my heart beat faster.

Fortunately, my mother's arrival saved me from having to respond. "Let's eat! Your father is just on his way down. Tom, will you open some wine? Do you boys want beer? I think we can do both," she said, heading to the wine fridge.

Plates overflowing, we all sat down to eat at the large round table in the breakfast nook. Sitting opposite Jim kept him in eyeshot, without being too obvious. The constant chatter could be overwhelming with such a large family, but he seemed to be easing into the evening. Luckily, with Chinese food, there was no silverware to worry about, and Jim was a pro with chopsticks. He had once told me there were only two restaurants in his little town. The diner that had opened circa 1910 as the railroad was being built, and a little Chinese restaurant that had moved in ten years ago whose owners, like so many immigrants, kept to themselves and devoted all their time to making their business a success. He'd become friends with the son, both driven in their studies and their need to succeed. The family had let them study in the restaurant after school, bringing bowls of rice and traditional dishes to the boys. It had made a real difference to Jim. His own family life was the opposite. Always strapped for cash, there was never enough in the icebox to feed a growing boy.

"So, Jim," my father's commanding voice boomed over the group, willing them to silence. "I hear you're studying for the LSAT. How are your grades and your practice tests?"

"I have a three point nine GPA and the practice tests have been going well. The actual LSAT is coming up in December."

"Jim is very driven," I interjected. "He spends all his free time studying."

"Let the man speak for himself, Abby." Devin

piped up. "He's all grown up now. You can let him leave the nest."

"Seriously, Devin?"

"Okay, kids, enough," my mother broke in.

"Well, as I was saying before all of your interruptions," my dad continued pointedly, "it takes a lot of drive to get through law school. Any idea where you'd like to go?"

"University of Chicago Law School is my top choice. It's a great school and Abby will be here." Jim smiled at me from across the table. "My chances of getting in seem decent, assuming the exam goes well."

"Well, I'm happy to write you an extra recommendation letter. It couldn't hurt and the Dean is an old friend of mine."

Jim looked startled and speechless. "Sir, that would be amazing. I don't know how to thank you."

"Just keep Abby happy and we will be all squared away. Now, is there any more Mongolian beef left?"

With that, the conversation shifted to the charity work my mother was doing that weekend. My gaze focused on Jim's surprised face. He gave me a genuine smile and my heart surged.

Later that evening, as we closed the door to my room, Jim put his arm around my waist and his face in my hair. "Thank you for inviting me, Abs. I didn't know family could be like this. My house was full of bickering around the clock. You guys actually like each other. It's amazing. And your dad…offering to write me a recommendation, I'm blown away. No one has ever been so kind."

"Jim, you're smart and have a great resume. You don't need my dad to get you where you're going."

"Well, it makes me feel a lot more confident in my chances."

I reached up on my tiptoes and kissed him. "My family is thrilled to get to know you. It makes me happy to see you getting along with everyone."

"Well, most of them. Devin definitely bumped into me on purpose when I was putting the pie in the oven. It's a good thing I've got these giant paws for hands or the damn pie would have exploded onto the floor."

"I'm sorry he was so rude toward both of us. He's super competitive but can't get his life together. The resentment comes out in childish ways and makes him into a moody jerk."

"Well, either way, our pie is definitely going to win."

"I don't know. My brothers' recipe for cherry pie is pretty tasty."

"Please, pecan pie trumps fruit pie any day of the week."

"Says the southern boy."

"And my word is law, Yankee girl, at least to you." Gently leaning in, his lips grazed my own. My mind drifted away as the warmth of the kiss crept down my body.

"Are you sure you don't want to break your rule about having sex in my parents' house?" My teeth nipped at his bottom lip.

"Absolutely. There's no way I could focus on anything but the creakiness of the mattress springs the whole time."

"Fair enough. Let's get ready for bed then. Tomorrow is going to be busy."

Going about our nighttime ritual, I realized how

familiar we had become to each other these past few months. I loved being in a couple, this couple. The future materialized before my eyes, every evening's end spent brushing our teeth, chatting over the day's events. I resolved to stop overanalyzing our relationship and accept what was right about us.

Chapter 2

In the morning, shouts of my brothers roughhousing in the TV room woke me from my slumber. Slipping out of bed, I threw on my bathrobe and padded down the hallway.

"Why are you guys shouting so early in the morning?"

"Seriously, Abby, it's nine a.m. You can sleep when you're dead. We have to get warmed up for a day of football." To accentuate his point, Devin tossed a football to the waiting arms of Will behind me.

"Oh my God, if you break a window, Mom is going to kill you," I huffed, feeling every bit the whiny little sister.

"Awe, you gonna tell Momma, baby?" taunted Devin, using my most hated childhood nickname.

"You're still my least favorite, Devin, just so you know." Grabbing the football from Will, I slammed it back to Devin and left.

Retreating back to my room, I paused at the doorway, struck by how absurdly attractive Jim looked sleeping, his back exposed above the comforter, his muscles chiseled from years of basketball. "Wake up, sleepyhead. It's getting late." My hand grazed his shoulder.

"Hey, dumpling." His arm reached up, pulling me down to the bed.

"Dumpling? That's a new one." I laughed.

His eyes flew open, confused. "Sorry, I didn't mean to call you that. Must have been dreaming."

"Who did you think you were talking to in this dream?" The nickname had been so specific it made me tense.

"Jeez, it's nine a.m. Your family is going to think I'm a bum. I better get dressed." He jumped out of bed and headed to the bathroom.

Baffled at his response, I shook it off and headed down to the kitchen to lend a hand. My cousin Lisa was bent over the sink, her elbow deep in a turkey.

"Find anything good in there?" I quipped.

"Funny girl. Nice of you to finally roll out of bed to come give me a little help." Lisa smiled back at me.

"It's so good to see you too." I gave her shoulders a squeeze. "Where would you have me start?"

"Why don't you start with the mushrooms and leeks for the stuffing?"

Walking over to the fridge, I began sorting through the overflowing refrigerator, looking for the leeks. Lisa looked over her shoulder and whispered, "I hear you brought a boy home. This is so exciting! Your mother has been gushing about this handsome guy all morning."

I groaned. "You sound like a teenager about to meet her favorite member of a boy band."

"Well, your mother also said he was polite and smart too, but handsome definitely got reiterated a few times."

"Oh, there you are. Did you and Jim sleep well?" my mother asked, joining us in the kitchen.

"Yes, thanks. You should have woken us up."

"It's fine. I'm sure you're exhausted after mid-terms."

"It seems you've been gossiping all morning, Mom."

"I was just giving Lisa an update on my children."

"Does that mean you and Dad approve of him?"

"Oh yes, your father is quite taken with Jim."

"Oh yes," Devin copied mockingly, standing at the kitchen door. "He's thinking about replacing some of his more worthless sons with the illustrious Jim Hardy."

"Devin! I don't appreciate your tone. You needn't be so caustic. This has nothing to do with you," my mother snapped. She was genuinely angry, a rare emotion for her.

Devin opened his mouth to reply, then quickly closed it and went out of the room.

I turned to my mother, exasperated. "What is his deal, anyway? He was such a jerk to me yesterday."

"Daddy told Devin there would be no more financial support from us while writing his great American novel. We're happy to have him move back home if he wants to work on it, otherwise it's time for a real job that actually pays his rent."

"Oh wow. That's huge. Good for Dad," I replied, surprised my father had taken such a tack. "Maybe it's the kick in his pants he needs to finally make something happen."

"Good morning!" Jim greeted everyone as he entered the room. "I'm so sorry I slept so late. Please put me to work. Potato peeling is a specialty of mine."

"Oh, wonderful. That's my least favorite job. Jim, meet Lisa, my niece."

Jim extended his hand as he walked around the

counter. "Lisa, it's a pleasure."

"Lisa is my sister's daughter, the one I told you about."

"My mother also passed from breast cancer. I'm sorry. It's an awful disease."

Lisa looked at Jim sympathetically. "So you understand. It was terrible, but I was so lucky to have Alice nearby. She was wonderful." Her eyes filled with tears. It had been so long ago, my recollections of it were interspersed with nightmares of a monster on the loose, snatching mothers and destroying lives. The fact that Jim had not mentioned his mother's death before now was still unnerving but the loss had clearly devastated him. His decision not to talk about it was one of self-preservation. It had nothing to do with me.

The hours passed in pleasant conversation as dinner came together. The ritual was comforting, lulling me away from any unsettled feelings. After the last of my tasks, I went upstairs to get ready. Coming back down, I saw my grandparents had arrived and were clustered in the hallway talking to Jim and my mother.

My grandfather stood erect. His powerful form was equally matched against Jim's. My grandmother sat in her wheelchair. She was immaculately coiffed with the cardigan of her twin sweater set arranged over her petite shoulders, but her expressionless face remained intent on the wall in front of her.

"Hello, Grandfather!" Bounding down the stairs, I leaped down, hugging him hard and breathing in his scent. "It's so good to see you." I kneeled and took my grandmother's hand in my own. "Hello, Grandmother, I'm your granddaughter, Abigail."

My grandmother looked up and smiled. "That's so

nice. You know, you have such a nice face, dear. Maybe you can help me. Do you know when they serve lunch on this flight?"

My mother stepped in and wheeled her mother to the kitchen. "Yes, ma'am, lunch is being served right now. Allow me to take you to your seat."

"She's getting worse," I said to no one in particular.

"Yes, she is. The doctor is not very positive about her progress. The nature of Alzheimer's, you know," Grandfather said, looking up at Jim and clapping him on the shoulder. "I've been talking to your fella here, Abigail, and I approve. He has a fine head on his shoulders. I'd better go check on your grandmother and maybe sneak a canapé or two."

Alone now, I looked at Jim and smiled. "So you've met Grandfather. What do you think?"

"I mean, he's great. I feel giddy. It's crazy that the senator is your grandfather. He's been behind every major piece of legislation for forty years."

"Well, he's still just Grandfather to me. I'm glad you got a chance to meet him. He means a lot to me."

Devin walked in, slightly unstable. "Aha, I see you've met the esteemed senator and worshiped at his alter no doubt." Miraculously the words were not slurred.

Jim's fist clenched. "I just introduced myself. You know, you should consider yourself lucky to have such a great man in the family. My grandfather was best known for his moonshine." He paused. "Then again, maybe you would have had more in common with him than you do the senator."

Devin's face grew dark and his chest puffed up, the

rage rolling off of him toward Jim. I cut in between them, immediately hit by the smell of alcohol on my brother's breath. "Relax! Cut it out. This is not the place to start one of your childish fights. Also, you stink of booze. It's not even two in the afternoon. Keep it together. Dad is going to kill you. Maybe you should go have some coffee. Or let's all go get something to eat in the kitchen. Mom made deviled eggs. You both like those. Maybe you could bond over that."

Devin's hostility toward Jim set off alarm bells in my head. He was a born curmudgeon, but his new predilection for plain cruelty was off-putting.

"Just ignore him," I whispered in Jim's ear as we headed toward the kitchen door. "Apparently, he and Dad had a big fight. He's just upset and taking it out on you."

"That's no excuse for it. If he wasn't your brother, I would have taken a swing at him."

In the kitchen, my grandfather looked up from cutting himself some cheese as we came in. "Jim, Anne was just telling me you're from Tennessee. It's a beautiful state. Did you grow up in Nashville, then?"

"No sir, I'm from a little town at the foot of the Smoky Mountains, not far from Knoxville."

"Will you be staying in Tennessee when you graduate, then?"

"No, sir, I'm actually hoping to come up here and pursue a law degree. I hope to practice law and then one day go into politics myself. Your career has been an inspiration, sir. You've made a real difference in people's lives. Hopefully someday I can accomplish even a fraction of that."

As my grandfather started to reply, Devin rolled his

eyes. Forcing eye contact with him, I mouthed "Follow me" and jerked my head toward the hallway.

Devin shrugged and started walking. I excused myself from the room and followed down the hall to my dad's study. Devin immediately began pouring a glass of scotch from the most expensive bottle on the bar cart, the one my father only opened on special occasions. "You know you're not supposed to be drinking that, and it's still early. Maybe you should stick with wine or beer."

"Whatever, Abby. You're such a little goody two shoes." He slammed the dark liquid back into his throat. "Seriously, Abby, what do you think this guy could possibly see in you? He's totally using you. His obsession with the great Lethican name is so obvious. You're nothing to him."

"You just met him. It's a little early to be passing judgment. He's just nervous meeting the family. He's so much more mature than any other guy I've dated. He's used his brains and his talent to fight to get this far and I respect him for it. Honestly, it feels like you're just jealous that the family has been so impressed with him." I softened my gaze. "I appreciate that you care, though frankly, I'm a little shocked by it. Don't you think I'm old enough to be the one who decides which man is right for me? Granted, maybe he's a little obsessed with our family. I'm not blind, but most people don't grow up hanging out with high-ranking politicians. If you started dating the daughter of the head coach of the Chicago Bears, and got to hang out with all the players, you might be a little starstruck too," I said, referencing my brothers' passion for football. "He's really into politics. This is exciting for him."

Devin took a deep breath and sat down, rubbing his temple. "Okay, you're right. I probably am being unfair. There's just something about this guy that rubs me the wrong way."

"Devin, you dislike everyone. You're a natural born grouch."

"Touché." His hand reflexively reached for the bottle again.

"Mom is going to be in tears if you are slurring your words at dinner. Can you slow down a little?"

He nodded. "You're right. Anyway, I hear screeching. Lisa's husband must have brought the kids. We'd better go wrangle them before something expensive gets broken."

Miraculously, dinner went off without a hitch. It was just as it should be, lots of food and laughter. Afterwards, my cousin Lisa and I took the dinner plates to the kitchen, hand washing the antique Wedgewood plates my mother only took out for special occasions. My father stuck his head in the kitchen to tell us everyone was ready for dessert.

We went back to the dining room. I looked around, expecting to see Jim. My mother noticed my quizzical expression. "That sweet boyfriend of yours noticed Nana had fallen asleep and offered to put her somewhere quiet so she could rest. He wheeled her into Dad's study. Why don't you go tell him we're ready to sample that delicious pie of his?"

Walking down the long hallway, my grandmother could be heard yelling loudly. I hurried my pace, stopping at the open door. Before me, Jim kneeled on the floor in front of my grandmother's wheelchair. His voice was calm, his words low and soothing.

"Now, Mrs. Lethican, you don't have anything to be afraid of. We're here at your son's home and we just had Thanksgiving dinner. I'm Jim, a special friend of your granddaughter, Abigail. You know, Abby has the most gorgeous blue eyes, and I do believe she inherited them from you. You must have been a great beauty in your day."

My grandmother stared at Jim, hypnotized. "Why, yes, I was. What did you say your name was?"

"Jim, ma'am."

"Have we met before?"

"No, ma'am. This is my first visit to Chicago, actually."

My heart warmed, both at his description of me and his kindness toward Nana. I cleared my throat. "Nana? Are you awake? Mom wants us to join her for pie."

"I love pie. Jim, do you love pie?"

"Indeed, I do. I'm excited to hear what you think of the pie I made. It's pecan."

"I like pecan. With ice cream, though."

"Abigail, did your mom buy ice cream?" Jim said, looking at me.

"She has ice cream and freshly made whipped cream all ready. You can have both if you like."

Jim stood up from his crouch. "We best get Nana back then before your brothers eat it all."

****

The next day, Jim and I got up and headed down to the kitchen. Tom was already taking down the extra chairs and tables. Jim offered to help.

"Oh, thanks, man. Listen, I wanted to talk to you.

My brothers and I are planning on going out for some ribs tonight and then meeting up with some people at the bars. We'd love for you to come along. Friday night after Thanksgiving is like the biggest going out night of the year in Chicago. We've got a lot of friends in town. Will is planning on having people over for drinks before we hit the bars. You in?"

Jim looked at me, unsure. "I'm not really sure what Abby has planned for us."

"Well, I thought we'd take the train downtown, do a little shopping, see the decorations, maybe stop by Millenium Park and go ice skating. Honestly, I hadn't gotten to dinner in my planning. I'm more than happy to head back to Winnetka on my own and you can go out with the boys."

"Are you sure? It doesn't seem right for me to abandon you like that."

"No, honestly, it'll be nice to spend some one-on-one time with my folks. Go! This is all part of having a relaxing weekend." I was glad my other brothers were making an effort to make Jim feel welcome. Hopefully their goodwill would rub off on Devin.

"Well, then, I'm looking forward to it, Tom. You think it would be better if the two of us carry that big table down the stairs?" They headed down to the basement, carefully angling the table to avoid scratching the wall.

Chapter 3

The mattress shifted heavily as Jim crawled into bed around three a.m., waking me. Within minutes, his snoring reverberated through the quiet room and the sour smell of alcohol and sweat assaulted my nostrils. Burying my face in the pillow, I tried to get back to sleep. Near dawn, exasperated, I gave up and put on my athletic clothes to go for a run. I thought about peeking into Tommy's room to coerce him into joining me. Tommy and I were both runners. In high school, we'd get up early before school and go running down Sheridan, looking for flashes of the sun breaking over Lake Michigan between the stately houses.

Heading toward the stairs, I saw Tommy sneaking up with a grin on his face. "Great minds think alike," he whispered.

"You're sure you're not too hungover?" I whispered back.

"Don't worry, I'll keep up." Reaching the kitchen, we spoke in normal voices.

"Seriously, Jim smells like he fell into a barrel. What happened last night? And why don't you look that bad?"

"Well, I think he was trying to win Devin over. Devin, being a jerk, kept plying him with whiskey all night. It was quite a sight. I don't think your guy drinks that much usually."

"No, not at all. He's either working out or studying. There's not a lot of time for socializing." We laced up our shoes and headed out. "Anything interesting happen? Did Devin behave?"

"Yeah, surprisingly. He was in a good mood. I guess he had some article accepted for publication and thinks it can buy him some time with Dad. Also, remember your little boyfriend, Bobby?"

The mention of Bob Greenwood brought back mixed emotions. He was a nice guy who had pursued me, hoping our friendship would blossom into something more. I hadn't been able to muster more than feelings of sisterly affection toward him.

"Anyway, he's living in New York, killing it trading and is dating this literal, swear to God, model and talking about getting married. He showed us some of the photo shoots she's done. Total knockout. Then Jim, who is fall down drunk at this point, says she looks just like a girl in his life."

"Wait, what? You don't mean me."

"No, he was slurring a lot but I think he said her name was Leah. You ever hear anything about her?"

"No," I said, frowning. Neither of us had volunteered much about our past relationships. Insecurity gripped me. "What did he say about her? He didn't say ex-girlfriend?"

"No, it was definitely present tense, but the guy was so bombed. He probably just misspoke."

Biting back tears, I stopped on the front walk. Had he been carrying on with someone else?

"Look, Abby, it's probably nothing. I'm making too big a deal of it. He was probably just trying to brag about bagging a hot chick, okay? Please, forget I said anything. Don't cry."

My jaw clenched. "Right, you're probably blowing this out of proportion. We spend so much time together. It would be hard for him to be sneaking around with another woman on campus right under my nose. Come on," I said, starting to run, "I'll race you to Tower Road Beach!"

"You're on. Just promise me we don't have to run up and down the hill when we get there."

We both took off, our bodies finding our old rhythm together. Pushing out the unsettling things Tom had said, my breath puffed out in a steady, soothing staccato. Of course, Jim had a past. We all did. In this moment, here with my family for the holidays, he was choosing me. His commitment to our relationship had been unflagging. It would be silly to bring it up and a breach of Tommy's trust. The drinking had made him nostalgic and brought up memories of an old girlfriend. I decided to let it go.

Chapter 4

Back at school, Jim and I settled into an idyllic routine of domesticity. His place became home base as it was closer to campus. After a particularly intense week school wise, I thought I would surprise him with a home cooked meal. My hands were full of groceries as I banged into the apartment. Hearing a voice from the bedroom, I assumed Jim was on the phone.

"Hey!" Jim exclaimed, coming into the kitchen. Rumpled in basketball shorts and a t-shirt, he looked like he'd just gotten out of bed.

"Hi. What are you up to? I thought I would make us dinner, maybe try my hand at home made meatballs. Are you okay? You look flushed."

"I'm okay, well maybe a little off. I didn't sleep so well last night, so I thought I would take a nap when my cousin, Lee, stopped by. She just needed to use the shower. The water is off at her place."

"Lee?"

"I could have sworn I mentioned Lee to you months ago. She's the one studying to be a paralegal. We're both so busy with school, it's hard to find a chance to meet up. You don't mind, do you?"

"No, of course not. I remember now. I would love to meet her. Maybe she could stay for dinner?"

"Ah, no, she mentioned plans. That's why she wanted a shower, to get ready for a date."

The door to the bedroom opened, and his cousin emerged. Encased in spandex, her fleshy hips were at odds with her trim waist. Her lips smiled, somehow managing to keep their perfect pout intact. She was blond and blue-eyed like me, but her wet hair was much longer, hanging down long past her enormous breasts, trapped unwilling beneath a sports bra. This was the girl from Jim's prom picture. It had hardly done her justice. She had been a child then. This was a woman who radiated raw sexuality.

Jim spoke quickly. "This is my dear, sweet cousin, Lee. We grew up together in Westin."

"So nice to meet you, Lee. How long have you been in Nashville?"

"Oh, years. I followed Jim out here after graduation. He was a year ahead of me in school. I'm studying to be a paralegal."

"That's wonderful." There was an awkward pause. She was still smiling but her displeased eyes kept glancing toward Jim. "Do you plan to stay here when you graduate?"

"It's undecided as of right now. I was just thinking it might be nice to follow Jim up to Chicago and get a job in the big city, now that University of Chicago offered him a place in the law school."

Jim's eyes stared back at her for a beat too long. He turned to me with a toothy grin. "Abby, you'll be happy to know, it's official. My acceptance letter came today. It's probably all due to your father's kindness. If you have any ideas for a thank you gift, I would appreciate it."

"Jim!" Bouncing on my tiptoes, my arms reached around his neck. "That's wonderful!!!! I'm so happy for you! For us!" I looked at Lee. "I'm not sure if you know, but I'm actually from Chicago, the suburbs anyway, and I'm planning on taking a job there after graduation."

"Oh, I know." Lee smiled. "I've heard all about you and your famous family. Well, I'm going to let you two celebrate in peace. So nice finally getting to put a face with a name," Lee said, grabbing her jacket.

"You too. Hopefully, we get to hang out again soon."

"Maybe," she said, brushing past me on her way out the door.

Later, after dinner, I'd insisted on running to the store to buy champagne to celebrate. Snuggling up on the couch, with our plastic solo cups fizzing, we started talking about the apartment we would get down in Hyde Park.

"This is wonderful, Jim. Getting a place of our own feels so grown-up. I'm so excited. It'll be nice for you too, once Lee comes up, right? You'll have family of your own there. There are so many members of the Lethican clan in Chicago, it can be a bit overwhelming."

"Lee, yeah, we hadn't really talked about what she would do after graduation. It was a surprise to hear she was planning on moving up."

"Why haven't we hung out with her before if she's been in Nashville this whole time? If you guys are so close, it would have been nice to meet her."

"Oh well, she lives clear across town. We just grab lunch at random times, that kind of thing. Honestly, since we started dating, I haven't been seeing her as much."

"Well, that makes me feel terrible. Why don't you give me her number and I'll text her. I'd love to get to know her. Oooh, you know, we should throw a party to celebrate. Maybe we could throw a dinner party. Do you think she'd come?"

"A dinner party, huh?" He grinned wickedly and continued on in a faux British accent. "The senator's granddaughter will be hosting a fabulous dinner for twelve. The silverware will be polished and the crystal glasses sparkling in the candlelight at her modest one-bedroom apartment."

"Very funny. I was thinking more like lasagna and paper plates."

"Right. I don't know if Lee will be interested but, when you figure out a date, let me know, and I'll shoot her a text. Now, if you don't mind, it's time for bed, little lady." He reached out his arms and lifted me up, as if I weighed nothing. Heading to the bedroom, all thoughts of Lee disappeared from my mind.

A few weeks later, we had set a date for the party. When I asked Jim if he had invited Lee, he said she wouldn't be available that day.

"Well, can we do something else with her? Why don't you give me her number?"

"I can't just give out her number."

"I'm her cousin's girlfriend, not some random weirdo."

"Okay, well, let me ask her next time I see her."

I frowned, wondering at Jim's caginess. Was he so desperate to escape his past, he would keep his family at a distance?

My suspicions were confirmed on campus the next day when I spied her walking across the street and ran after her.

"Lee! Hey, how are you?"

She looked up at me, surprised, nervously glancing behind her. "Hey, Abby. How are you?"

"Is everything all right?" I asked.

"Yeah, it's fine. I'm just worried about something. I stopped by Jim's place to talk about it but he couldn't really help." Her head bobbed toward Jim's apartment, just a few blocks away.

She seemed reluctant to make eye contact. Feeling awkward, my instinct was to fill the silence. "Well, I'm sorry you can't come to the dinner party, but maybe we could hang out sometime, just the two of us. I'd love to get to know you better. I asked Jim for your number, but he said he wanted to ask you first if it was okay…"

"Dinner party?" She seemed surprised.

"Yes, on Friday, at Jim's place, to celebrate his acceptance to law school."

"Dinner party. Right, you know my plans just got canceled so I can come after all. Isn't this a happy coincidence running into you? Do you have your phone on you? Shoot me a text with the details and we'll be good to go."

Obediently, I popped the number into my phone. "Well, that's great. I'm glad you can come."

She started to walk away, then paused, glancing over her shoulder to flash me a cloying smile. "Sounds good. You know, why don't we not tell Jim about my change of plans. It'll make it a fun surprise."

"Sure. If that's what you want." A niggling feeling took hold. Had she intentionally not been invited because Jim was embarrassed of her? She was beautiful, but her clothes were trashy and worn. She hardly fit in with the polished persona Jim had tried to present to his college friends. Shaking off such a shallow thought, I hoped Jim would not be angry at his surprise.

****

The day of the party found me a bundle of nerves. Maintaining my silence about inviting Lee had me nervous about angering Jim. His temper was usually under control, but once released, it could be terrifying. There was always tension beneath his surface, waiting to break free.

Jim set the table as I finished up the salad, the lasagna already in the oven.

"How many people did you say?"

"Twelve." I smiled. "Isn't that what you said would make the perfect number for a dinner party?"

"Who all is coming?"

"The usual, you'll see. We might even have a surprise guest or two."

A knock on the door announced the arrival of the first guests. Jim brought his basketball friends into the kitchen. "Hey, Abby, it smells good in here."

"Thanks. Do you want a beer?" Gesturing toward the fridge, I straightened up, slightly intimidated by all the tall bodies surrounding me.

"So, Abby, you got any single girlfriends coming? *Cute* single girlfriends?"

"There are definitely some single girls coming." I smiled.

"Hello, anyone here?" Lee called from the front door.

"In the kitchen," I responded. Jim's face froze, his death stare pointed at me. As Lee waltzed into the kitchen in a skintight, low cut dress, that look turned into pure rage.

"Lee," Jim said, his voice steely. "What are you doing here?"

One of Jim's friends gave out a low whistle. "Well, Abby, this better be one of the single girls you were talking about."

Tension emanated between Lee and Jim. Nervously swallowing, I responded, "Ha, you know, I don't actually know if Lee is single. Lee is Jim's cousin. Have you guys not met her before?"

"No, ma'am. I'm Robert." Jim's friend reached out his hand with an appreciative wink.

"Surprise, Jim. I ran into Lee on campus and convinced her to join us tonight. Isn't that fun?" I finished lamely.

"Yes, very fun. Lee, can I speak to you a minute in the bedroom?" Jim grabbed Lee's elbow and dragged her away.

"Well, this party certainly got more exciting. There's no way she goes to school here, right? I definitely would have noticed her," Robert said to me.

"No, not here, but somewhere in Nashville. She's studying to be a paralegal. Will you excuse me?" Walking toward the bedroom, I hoped to rein Jim in and shoulder the blame.

The door to the bedroom was ajar. Jim's voice came out like a hiss. "What the hell were you thinking coming here in that outfit no less?"

"Your *girlfriend* invited me." Sarcasm dripped from the word girlfriend.

My knock on the door was firm. "Jim, we have guests. She's right. I invited her. If you want to be angry, be angry at me. I meant this as a pleasant surprise, not whatever this is." My hand waved back and forth between the two of them.

He took a deep breath. "You're right. I'm sorry. I was just caught off guard. We better get back to the party."

Jim walked past me. As Lee went past, I felt the need to apologize. "I didn't mean to cause any trouble between the two of you."

"It's fine. He's always been a bit cagey with his family."

"What do you mean?"

"He's just protective. Now, if you'll excuse me, I am going to go get acquainted with that friend of yours, Robert." She pulled down on her dress, pushed her cleavage up, and shimmied back to the kitchen.

The rest of dinner was spent with Jim in an ill humor, glowering across the table at Lee. Robert ate up her shameless flirting, hook, line and sinker. It was unclear to me if she was interested in him, or just trying to get Jim's goat, though both could be true.

After dinner, Lucy followed me into the kitchen, carrying dirty plates. "That's Jim's cousin? I feel so intimately acquainted with her."

"What do you mean?" My eyebrows furrowed.

"I mean, that dress. It doesn't leave a lot to the imagination. Poor Robert didn't know what hit him."

"What do you think of her otherwise? Jim was so angry that I invited her. I wish I hadn't. It seemed like the nice thing to do at the time. She's definitely laying it on thick with the sultry kitten act."

"Yeah, I'm not really a fan. Maybe Jim didn't want her here because she always throws herself at his friends. She seems messy."

"Maybe she gets like this when she drinks? I've only met her once before."

Through the door, we watched Lee standing up slowly, her hand on Robert's shoulder. Her pillowy cleavage grazed him as she straightened, whispering something in his ear that brought a smile to his face.

After dinner, our friends stayed to chat for a bit, but finally, with midnight approaching, they began to say their goodbyes.

Lee stood up, wobbly on her high heels. "Robert, would you be a total sweetheart and walk me home?" Her voice came out in a purr.

With a lascivious grin plastered on his face, Robert nearly tripped over his own feet racing to the door. "I'd like that very much. Jim, my man, I promise to deliver her safely to her door. Abigail, the food was delicious. Definitely beats the dining hall. See you guys later."

Soon the others followed and we were alone. My mouth opened in apology and Jim raised his hand to stop me. "Don't start, Abby."

"I just want to know if you're okay. I am really sorry for inviting her. How was I to know she'd get wasted and throw herself at your friends?"

He shook his head, a look of quiet sorrow clouding his face. "She's just like that sometimes. You never know who you're going to get. But when there're men around, she really likes the attention, you know? She just can't help herself. I don't want you becoming friends with her, Abby. She can be very manipulative and I don't want her to have any kind of hold over you. You're so gullible sometimes."

My feathers ruffled at such a set down. "Gullible?

My kindness does not make me gullible. I just like to see the best in people." Breathing in slowly, I tried to reframe the conversation, hoping to avoid a fight this late in the evening. "That's fine. You're right. We don't have a lot in common. You're always welcome to invite her over, but I won't actively try to be friends."

He looked at me, shaking his head. "Oh, Abby, why is everything so complicated sometimes?"

"It's not as bad as all that."

"You don't know the half of it." Walking toward me, he rested his chin on top of my head. "I'm exhausted. Can we just go to sleep?"

****

A few weeks later, I was getting lunch at the coffee shop on campus when Robert came in. "Hey, I saw you through the window. Just thought I'd say hi."

The gesture surprised me. Though never rude, Robert had always seemed indifferent to my presence. "Hey, good to see you. Thanks again for coming, and for offering to take Lee home."

"You know, now that you mention it, that's kind of what I want to talk to you about."

"About Lee? I don't really know her at all."

"Okay, I'm just wondering, has she said anything about me?" Robert asked.

"I haven't seen her since the party and Jim hasn't mentioned it. Why?"

"Nothing, we just, we had an amazing night together after the dinner, if you know what I mean." He looked down at me slyly through his lashes. "And then nothing. Every time I text her, she blows me off or makes an excuse. I just don't get it."

"Why don't you ask Jim? He'd know better than

me. They just had dinner together last week."

"I tried to ask him once, but he's so damn prickly about her. Ah, well, it was worth a try. See you later, Abby."

It seemed Lee had been using Robert to get to Jim, no doubt upset he hadn't invited her himself. Or maybe she had woken up hungover, regretting the night. It wasn't impossible that Robert had overestimated his charms. Either way, Jim had made it clear Lee was none of my business.

Chapter 5

The last few weeks of school sped by. After graduation, we headed up to Chicago, to an adorable vintage apartment in Hyde Park, on Chicago's South Side so Jim could be close to the law school. Starting my new job, I commuted every day, taking the bus downtown, and did a fair amount of traveling for work. We didn't socialize a lot. Jim was focused on school. There were a few other couples we would see who were also students at the law school.

After Lee graduated, she had moved to Chicago as planned but was living on the North side. Jim would occasionally see her for dinner when I was out of town for work, but mostly we were home bodies. After work, I was happiest puttering around my kitchen, or doing a load of laundry while Jim spent his time head bent over law books on the kitchen table. The years flew by. They were some of my happiest. After law school, Jim joined the top tier firm at which he had interned. We moved downtown so Jim would be close to work. With Jim always at the office, we didn't get a chance to see each other as much. Sometimes, after work, I would go to the gym and then walk over to his office if he could get away for a quick bite, before heading back up for a long night. Despite my efforts, it was a struggle to stay connected. His whole existence revolved around his job.

Occasionally, he had dinner with Lee, but most of his friends from law school were in similar positions of near constant work and had dropped out his life. Lonely for the first time in my life, our relationship seemed unsustainable in its current state. After four years, I was dodging constant inquiries from my family about getting married. It seemed trite to bother him about getting engaged, my need for him to validate his feelings with a ring. Any intimacy between us had disappeared, his need for sleep more pressing than sex.

With these thoughts churning inside me, I'd scheduled dinner with Lucy at a restaurant not far from Jim's work. She was in town for a conference and I was really looking forward to unburdening myself to an old friend. Taking the longer route to the restaurant past Jim's office building on the off chance he might be doing a coffee run, I saw the back of his head towering above the others, going through the revolving doors. Outside the door, slowly walking toward me in tears, was Lee, oblivious to my presence.

"Lee, are you okay? What happened?"

"Oh god, it's you." Her head shook erratically. "Sorry. I didn't expect to see you here."

"I was headed to dinner down the block. Do you need help? Can I get you an Uber?"

She looked at me, her eyes narrowing with suspicion. "No thanks, I need to walk." She turned quickly and headed the opposite direction.

Bewildered, I texted Jim. —*I just saw Lee, is everything okay?*—

The dots beat out in response. —*She's fine. Can't talk now.*—

Shaking off the feeling of unease that had taken

hold, I walked to the restaurant to meet Lucy, grateful for a sensible sounding board. "The weirdest thing just happened." Eagerly, I explained the run in with Lee on the street.

"Wait, this is the one that looks like a pinup model? Maybe she had too many dates tonight and couldn't pick one."

"Lucy, you're awful and I love you for it. But seriously, that's not nice. She was genuinely distressed. She's usually so detached and cool. It was bizarre."

"Well, maybe you should call her. You might not be the closest of friends but she is Jim's family."

"You're right. Maybe when she calms down, she'll want to talk." The mention of Jim brought back all the concerns about my relationship. The words came tumbling out. "Not to dump everything on you, but, Lucy, the time we were living in Hyde Park was amazing. We were both working hard obviously, but it felt like a team. We spent time together as a couple, whether it was watching Netflix or even just reading together in bed. Through all of it, we were connected. Now, I just don't know. He's either never home, or responds with one-word answers. Is it time for me to push for more in our relationship when it's clear that he's crazy busy? I can't help feeling lonely but don't know what to do about it without feeling like a shrew. What do you think?"

She sighed. "Oh, Abby, you know how I feel about it. You've never been well-suited. You shouldn't be with someone who is so self-involved and can't appreciate you as a person. It's like you're his house manager. You just make his life run smoothly. The man you choose should love you for your sense of humor and your kindness, someone who's going to tell you you're beautiful every day, and make time for you. You're the priority. With Jim, it's always Jim and what have you done for me lately."

Nodding slowly, the truth behind the words began to seep in. "We've been together so long. Who am I without him, and what does being alone even look like as an adult? The thought of spending my evenings on a dating app or grabbing drinks with strange men just makes me cringe."

"You're twenty-five. You have your whole life ahead of you. There's plenty of time to figure it out. You might just feel a lot less lonely being out of a relationship than in this one."

That evening, at home getting ready for bed, by myself as always, I tried to read myself to sleep but couldn't concentrate. Lucy's words kept playing over in my head. What would an evening as a single girl look like? Would I be coming home from a date right now, or a night out with girlfriends instead of sitting around nervously, hoping for a five-minute chat with Jim before he declared he was dead on his feet. Lulled to sleep mulling over my options, a dip in the mattress woke me.

"Jim. What time is it?" My mouth felt dry trying to articulate the words.

"Late. It's about three a.m."

"Three? You haven't been at work this whole time, have you?"

"No, no…I had to go see Lee."

"How's she doing? Can you tell me what's going on…if it's not too personal, of course…"

Jim looked down at his hands and then began

cracking his knuckles. It was a habit when he was unsure of himself or nervous. "She's pregnant."

"Oh my goodness, I didn't know she was dating anyone."

"Well, she's not really…she, ugh…well I don't want you to judge her, Abby, but she got involved with one of the married partners at her firm." He paused, letting the words sink in. "She really fell hard for him. It was not a planned pregnancy obviously, at least I don't think it was. Maybe she thought she could entrap him…" His voice sounded far away, lost in thought. "If that was the idea, it didn't go her way. She should have known better." The lamp on the nightstand clicked on, blinding me. "I offered to take her to Planned Parenthood, but you know, she was raised Catholic and she's being unreasonable. She says she's having the baby no matter what."

"Well, what did the guy say?"

"He does not want to be recognized as the father and she's afraid of losing her job if she makes a big deal about this."

"That's awful." Angry, I sat up in bed. "It's ridiculous that as women, we still fall victim to this. Do you really think she could get fired?"

"It's possible. I offered to try and get her a job at my firm. That way she could start fresh, make the move before she's showing. When her pregnancy starts to show, she can just say she broke up with her boyfriend and decided to keep the baby. Listen, Abby," he reached for my hand. "I told her I would help her out financially as much as possible. Being a single mother is hard and I can't let her do it alone. This kid can't grow up feeling like he doesn't have a father. It's crazy, but I've known Lee my whole life, if she's having this baby, I need to be a part of his life."

"No, absolutely, she's family." I was startled by the fervor and raw emotion in his eyes, but also touched. Jim was a good man to care so much, to be so concerned for this unborn child. "I'm happy to help too. Daycare pickup if she's working late, babysitting if she needs some time to herself…this is your decision and it's absolutely the right one, and I support you. I love you, Jim." My concerns about our relationship evaporated. I felt one with him again, taking on this new challenge.

"Abby, you're the best. I am so grateful to have met you. You are my lucky star, Abby." He kissed me. "I didn't really plan this, and as proposals go, it's pretty lame, but will you marry me?"

My jaw went slack. "Are you serious? Are you sure?"

"Yes! Of course, I'm sure. I even looked at some rings online, but work has been too crazy for me to go in and look at them in person. Come on, say yes, Abby."

My heart was pounding. "Yes, absolutely. I don't need a fancy ring, Jim. This is more than enough. I love you."

"Well, you'll get your fancy ring anyway, Abigail, but all told, it's probably better you help pick it. I have no idea what women like."

"That's not fair! The jewelry you bought me is beautiful!" My wrist swiveled back and forth, modeling the bracelet he'd given me last Christmas.

"Well, Lee may have helped me just a bit."

His breath was hot against my neck and I arched

my back, welcoming his caresses. Happiness flowed through my body, pushing out the nagging feeling that he had just proposed without mentioning the three little words, "I love you." He'd never directly said the words. When pressed in the past, he would admonish me. "Abby, you know how I feel about you. My actions speak louder than words." His ready-made excuses included growing up in a family that was not openly affectionate. His proposal would have to be enough.

That weekend, we had brunch with my parents and told them the good news. Jim was concerned he should have asked my dad first for my hand in marriage, but my family was thrilled, even without the old-fashioned nod. My suggestion that Lee might join us for brunch now that we were all going to be family fell on deaf ears. Jim insisted it would be best not to flaunt our happiness in light of her recent predicament. I understood his perspective, but it left me in an awkward position with her. It seemed to me that I could use this crisis to pull closer to her and cut a swathe through her prickliness.

I decided to text her on my own.

—*Hey Lee, it's Abby. Can I stop by tonight and talk to you? Maybe I could pick up takeout?*—

Her reply came almost instantly. —*Sure, why not.*—

Before going up to Lee's apartment in Lakeview, I stopped at my favorite Thai place and picked up some pad see ew, chicken with vegetables, and egg rolls, hoping she would find at least some of it appetizing. On the drive, it occurred to me she might not be aware that Jim had shared her situation. It would be best to be upfront and let her know she had my full support.

She buzzed me in and I climbed up the flight of stairs to her apartment, my hands full with bags. At the top of the landing, Lee stood with the door already open, pale and tired, but looking beautiful and very young. It seemed unpardonable that a man would abandon a woman during such a time, but she held her head high as she invited me in.

"What do you need to talk to me about, Abby?" Her face remained motionless, watching. She seemed to be prepared to do battle. Did she think I came here to condescend to her?

"Jim told me everything, and I'm so sorry, Lee. I just want you to know how much I respect you for keeping the baby."

"Everything, eh? Jim told you everything? Oh really. And what would 'everything' be exactly?" Her icy voice cut through me, sharp and unforgiving.

"Jim told me you were pregnant. He said that the father was a lawyer in your practice who was married and refused to take responsibility for the baby. I know Jim offered to help you financially and that is fine with me. Now that we are going to be family, I want you to think of me as a bonus aunt. I've talked to Jim. After the wedding, we will be looking to buy a house. We're planning to move up here, nearby to help out with daycare pickups, babysitting, or trips to the park to give you some time to yourself. I can't imagine being a single mother. You're so brave." My words had not had the effect I intended. Her shoulders tensed up and the vein near her eye twitched.

"After the wedding?" The tension in her voice was thick.

"Yes, I'm sorry. Did Jim not tell you? He

proposed. We're getting married! We haven't really had time to think about when the wedding is going to be. Maybe this summer? With so much family, it's probably going to be a big wedding but we will try to keep it simple." Her silence goaded me on. "I don't want you to be embarrassed about your situation. It is awful, absolutely awful that a man would lie and not take responsibility when there is a child's life involved. I'm so sorry you're dealing with this."

"Awful. Just awful. Isn't it, though?" Her eyes twinkled at me. "Truly the man was a monster and I just didn't see it. Must have been taken in by his charm. It happens to a lot of women though, right, Abigail?"

"It's completely understandable. Men can be so persuasive sometimes." The vibe in the room remained awkward as she gave me a glassy-eyed stare. "Let me know if there's anything I can do for you, like drive you to doctor visits or help paint the baby's room. Seriously, I'd like to be friends if you'll let me."

Lee took a deep breath. "That's mighty nice of you. You know, I'm feeling a little overwhelmed, and truth be told, morning sickness seems to be hitting me at all hours. Do you mind if we reschedule this little get together?"

I forced a smile. "Yes, of course. Just text me if you need anything. Do you want me to leave the food?"

"No, ma'am. I am finding the smell a little much. Why don't you take it home to that precious fiancé of yours?"

"Understood. Well, text me if you need anything." Tripping over the doorstep, I hurried out, glad our meeting had come to an end. Her stony gaze had been unnerving. It was no surprise. Lee had always struck me as a proud woman. Perhaps she'd gambled that she would have the upper hand if she was with child. With her great beauty and a baby on the way, she may have thought the man would actually leave his wife, though it was unkind to think it had been on purpose. It was hard to have any grace in this situation.

Driving back downtown, the smell of fried food permeated through the car. It struck me as strange that Jim hadn't yet bothered to mention our engagement. It was possible he was looking for a better time, or to tell her in person. Her surprise that we would be considering marriage after all these years wounded me, as if she'd been expecting Jim to tire of me long before there were wedding bells.

Once we started the wedding planning, the event turned into a carnival of epic proportions and we ended up pushing the wedding back to the following winter. The marriage of a senator's daughter would qualify as a big event and had to be planned with care and pomp. The wedding planner and my mother had a constant flow of crazy plans they had hatched up, hell-bent on making this the farthest thing from simple imaginable.

A few months before the big day, Jim and I were out to brunch, waiting for some friends. I was trying to fill him in on the recent changes to the theme, his eyes glazing over with every word out of my mouth. It struck me he might not want a big wedding. His family was likely not coming. I had met his father at his respective college and law school graduations. A quiet man, he hadn't spoken much either time before Jim had ushered him away to spend 'one on one' time with him. My mother's invitations to dinner were invariably declined by Jim, claiming his father was a recluse and any social event would be stress inducing. Jim told me his father didn't want to come up for the wedding, which I found heartbreaking, but clearly, though bothered by it, Jim had no desire to discuss it.

It suddenly occurred to me that this wedding was getting away from us. It was foolish and selfish of me to have such an extravagant event when most of the guests would be from my family. "Jim, I'm so sorry. I'd never even asked you if you wanted a wedding, let alone such a circus. It was so thoughtless of me. Why don't we elope? We can go to Vegas. Or we can go to city hall and just head out on our honeymoon. You really don't have to do this for me."

"Wait, what the hell are you talking about? Why would we skip having a wedding?"

"I just thought you seem so bored whenever I talk about it."

"Of course it's boring. I have other things to think about than table linens. That doesn't mean I am not looking forward to the amazing wedding you and your mother are orchestrating. I just don't have a lot to add to it. *Our wedding* is important." He touched my engagement ring, centering the perfect oval cut diamond on my finger.

"Even if it's mostly my family?"

"It's not mostly your family. It's a lot of our friends, and there are a lot of important people from work on the guest list. It will be very beneficial to my career to have some of the partners rubbing elbows with my father-in-law, the senator."

His tone chilled me to my core. Jim was looking at our wedding as a way to vault his position at work. It hadn't occurred to me, though in reality, as a politician's daughter, that had been very naïve of me. Life was always an exchange of goods and services, an opportunity to do a favor and be favored in return at a later date.

"Of course. How foolish of me. The optics of an elopement would not be ideal for your career. Obviously, there are more people involved than just me."

Jim's phone buzzed. "Oh my God, it's happening. Lee is in labor. I got to go, Abby. I said I'd drive her to the hospital." He stood up and kissed the top of my head. "I'll call you later."

The heat shimmered on the sidewalk through the window as my fiancé sprinted out into the warm summer day to hold another woman's hand during her labor. The intimacy of the event uncoiled a wave of jealousy around my heart, though my head knew his actions to be noble. She was alone. It was the decent thing to do. He would spin his selflessness toward Lee to his colleagues to put himself in a good light. Apparently, people had been surprised when Lee had started showing almost immediately after taking the job at his firm. Jim had stepped in, quick to explain she had needed the work, forced into the role of single motherhood. With broad strokes, Jim's adaptation painted him as the hero, helping his little cousin out. Our motives are not always straightforward in life.

David was born early the next morning. My visit to the hospital was delayed until the afternoon to give them both time to rest. Despite the awkwardness with Lee, and her unwillingness to let me into her life, I hoped this little boy would make her softer. Children were a blessing and I looked forward to being a part of his life. Spending time with the both of them might just be the bridge we needed to become closer.

Getting off the elevator, I headed down the hallway. In front of her room, my hand wavered before knocking, worried that Lee might be getting some needed rest. I pulled my hand back and started digging into my purse, looking for my phone to text Jim. The door was slightly ajar and Jim and Lee's voices drifted toward me, so I pushed the door open wide.

"Lee, you can't do this. I will not support you if you do this," Jim said heatedly.

Jim's startled and angry face swung toward me.

"Hey, guys. Congratulations. I didn't know whether to bring flowers but figured you had enough to carry home with this little guy. How are you feeling, Lee? He's gorgeous!" I smiled, ignoring the tension radiating between them.

Lee looked over at me. "Oh, it's you. I feel all right, I guess. Pretty sure I never want to go through labor again though. Do you want to hold him?" She looked over at Jim, a smirk on her face.

The clear animosity in her voice unnerved me but I thought it best to ignore it. "Yes, I'd love to. David is such a great name. Does he have a middle name yet?"

"James, of course. It's my way of saying thank you to Jim, for *everything*." Her emphasis on the word 'everything' was riddled with sarcasm.

"That's so nice of you. You must be so in love with him already. He's such a big boy!"

"I have to get going. I have briefs I need to read. Lee, I'm glad it's over. You've given birth to a beautiful son." He took her hand, and bent over and kissed it. A look passed between them and she smiled at him. Tears glistened in her eyes.

"Yes, he's beautiful. Okay, we'll see you when you come to take us home, right?"

"You bet. I'll bring your car and install the car seat for you. Your car keys are in my pocket." He patted his jeans and nodded in my direction. "Abby, I'll see you at home."

Jim brushed past me with a quick kiss on the cheek and I sat next to Lee with the baby still in my arms. "You know, if you're tired, I can go, or I can take him and push him around the floor. My day is wide open if you need me."

"No! Please, don't take him. I don't mind you holding him, but can you just stay here?" Lee suddenly looked very small and very tired.

"Sure, you got it. Why don't you sleep, and I'll wake you if he gets hungry."

Lee quickly nodded off and I looked down at the little boy. For a second, he looked a bit like Jim. No doubt the two of them took after the same long gone ancestor. As he screwed up his little face, I was reminded that all babies look a little alike, and also like Winston Churchill. My maternal urges exploded with full force while holding the newborn. Would Jim want to start trying for our own children after the wedding? We'd already started looking at a few houses in Lee's neighborhood. It was a cute part of the city, with lots of parks and young families. There were shops and restaurants with stroller parking. It would be a nice place to raise a family. David could grow up with cousins and maybe feel a little less lonely. I couldn't imagine being an only child. My life had always been full of commotion and friendship and the animosity of my siblings, and every minute of it had been wonderful.

After an hour or so, the doctor came in to check on the baby. I woke Lee up and turned the baby over to her. "He's perfect. I'm going now but text me if you need anything, okay?" I gave the bed an awkward pat.

Back at our apartment, Jim had his work spread out over the dining room table. "I think we definitely need to get you a nice, large office when we move." My nose wrinkled at the mess.

"That would be good. I always feel like everything is organized just the way I want, then it's time to clean up for dinner."

"Speaking of, any requests? Do you just want to get carry out?"

"Actually, I might head back to the hospital and bring Lee something. She's probably feeling pretty alone right now. Babies aren't the best conversationalists. And I'd like to see David some more."

"You're really going above and beyond for her. It's really inspiring."

He looked at me warily. "Am I? You know, I'm planning on seeing him often. Are you going to be jealous of the time I spend with them?"

"I don't know that jealous is the right word. It would bother me if I wasn't included in that time, at least part of the time. In my head, we should be a package deal, like an aunt and uncle to little David, if you will."

"Right. Not to ruffle your feathers, but you and Lee don't always get along. She might not take kindly to you being there all the time."

"Does she not like me?" His words hurt, though

68

her coolness had always suggested some animosity toward me.

"She likes you fine, but I just don't think she considers you a good friend. Lee's very closed off. She had a hard childhood, and doesn't really trust people. Her father was a real piece of work. He was not a kind man. Her mother is very rigid and moralizing. God and righteousness is all that counts in her book."

I realized how little Jim had spoken of Lee's past. It hadn't occurred to me to ask. So intimidated by Lee's model good looks, I had assumed her life had been easy. Or perhaps it was my own easy upbringing that caused me to assume people had been raised with love and kindness, rather than hate and hardness.

"Well, hopefully our marriage can bring us all closer. You know, I've barely spent time with any of your family and I would like to rectify that by thinking of Lee as family." There was a pause and Jim looked back down at his work. My hand trailed around the edge of the table, hoping my next question wouldn't set him off. "What were you two arguing about when I walked in?"

"Excuse me?"

"You said you wouldn't support her. What did you mean?"

"That's none of your business, Abigail. Do you make a habit of eavesdropping on all my conversations?" The words were embossed with a steely edge.

"I'm sorry, it just seemed so threatening. It didn't seem right to be badgering her so soon after she had gone through labor. Please don't be mad at me," I implored.

Jim rubbed his jaw and breathed deeply. "I guess I can tell you. Don't you dare ever to bring it up to Lee, though." My forehead furrowed, but I nodded, happy to be let in. "She wanted to name the father on the birth certificate. I thought it was a bad idea. It would be better for everyone concerned for her to move on from him."

"That's crazy though. A, it's her child, Jim. She can do as she wants. B, she really should be suing him for some sort of child support. There are DNA tests, you know. It would force his hand."

"Ahh, that's the thing. He's offered to send her some monthly stipend as long as she doesn't reveal his involvement. Putting his name on the birth certificate could jeopardize that for her."

My head was spinning. "So she's just supposed to trust him to do the right thing? You're a lawyer— shouldn't you advise her to have it in writing?"

"It's a special situation, Abby. This is what I think is for the best and it really is none of your business." He took a breath and reached for my hand. "And I appreciate you wanting to consider Lee family. Maybe we could set up a weekly dinner with her and David when the boy is a little older. Plus, we're still planning on moving up to Lakeview, right? Proximity to you might soften her up a bit."

Jim was clearly trying to redirect my indignation. In the spirit of peace, I let him. "Right. As soon as we get through the wedding, I'll start looking for a house. We should sit down at some point soon and finalize the invitations. January is not that far off."

We'd decided on a Winter Wonderland themed wedding. Jim had wanted to push the wedding back after David's birth and January seemed a perfect time for a wedding, people's calendars being so empty after the rush of the holidays.

"Of course. Now, if you don't mind, I need to get back to work."

"Sure, I should go for a run, anyway." Without a backward glance, still biting my tongue, I left him to his work.

Chapter 6

Summer was drawing to a close and, after receiving zero responses to my text messages, I had steered clear of Lee. Jim had continued to visit her on the weekends without me. With the added trips to the north side, and Jim's intensive work schedule, we again began to see each other so infrequently, I wondered if I would recognize him when our wedding day came. So much of the little time we had together was spent going over wedding details. None of my girlfriends had ever mentioned how alienating planning a wedding with your fiancé could be. He was not interested in the process, but still did not trust me with the details. The wedding in his mind was a social statement—the more expensive the better—especially as my parents had given us carte blanche with the bill. Desperate to have the planning finally done, I capitulated to all his demands.

The one thing that was my own was dress shopping. While uncertain about my vision of the perfect dress, I did know my mother was looking forward to it and would be full of opinions. We set a date to go out. My cousin Lisa would join us and my friend Lucy, my maid of honor, was flying in for it. On a last-minute whim, I texted Lee and asked her to join us. Jim had floated the idea that David could be included in the wedding. It would give us the requisite adorable child in a pint-sized suit the old ladies loved to coo at carried down the aisle. If Lee was willing to join us, she and Lucy could plan coordinating dresses, and David could make his entrance on Lee's arm. I had no other bridesmaids. Jim had decided his friend, Robert, from college would be his best man. My brothers were thrilled not to have to walk down the aisle, though my mother was insisting they all be outfitted in tuxedos.

The day of the big shopping excursion had arrived, and though there had been no formal response from Lee, she was at the dress salon when we arrived. She had brought David and he was sitting up like a little king in his stroller, the clerks at the store gushing baby talk into his cherubic face. "Lee! I'm so glad you could make it." She gave me a faux cheek kiss.

"Since I am always going about life backwards, I thought I could live vicariously through you. It's nice of you to include us. Thank you."

She had so frequently avoided me that her kind words came as a surprise. Warmed by the sentiment, I decided to use it to my advantage. Jim had skirted around the question of whether his father was coming to the wedding and Lee, in her good mood, might be able to give me a straight answer.

"Listen, Lee, before everyone else comes, do you know if Jim's dad is coming? Every time I bring it up, Jim just dismisses me and tells me that his dad isn't sure. Do you know what the holdup is? If it's the cost of flying up or finding a place to stay, my family would be happy to help out."

Lee looked at me suspiciously and then looked down at David. "Honestly, it's more complicated than that. Jim's dad has a hard time getting around since his accident. He doesn't get out much. It would probably be a lot for him. Also…" She paused and looked down. "He and my mother talk sometimes. Jim's mom and my mom were sisters, you know."

"No, actually, I didn't realize you were first cousins. It was silly of me not to have asked."

"Well, my momma, she's a very strict Catholic. She, umm…" Tears filled her eyes. "This may come off as strange, but, I never told her about David. We don't talk that often, and she's always so critical. If she thought I'd had a child out of wedlock, she would disown me." Her face paled in anticipation of my censure.

"Oh, Lee, I'm so sorry. That's terrible. You're afraid that if Jim's dad comes, he'll tell your mother. David is such a sweet boy, and you're a wonderful mother. You have nothing to be ashamed of." I hugged her, and for the first time in our relationship, she hugged me back. My mother approached us from the back of the store. "Listen, I'll just assume Jim's dad isn't coming and stop pushing him about it, ok? This will stay between us. It's important for you to feel comfortable at our wedding. You are Jim's closest family."

Lucy, Lisa and my mother sat down on a nearby couch as the sales assistant came forward to ask me what my perfect dress looked like before she started pulling samples. "Um, white and poofy?" My nose scrunched up in confusion.

My mother shook her head and reached into her cavernous bag. A stack of bridal magazines came out, peppered with post-it notes between the pages. "Let's sit down and I'll show you what *we* were thinking." She strode off ahead of us.

My lips curled up in a tight smile. "See, my mother can be a little overbearing sometimes too."

She shook her head at me and headed over to the seating area.

After hours of dress shopping followed by a late lunch, which Lee begged out of, saying it was time for David's nap, I headed back to our condo downtown. I was excited to tell Jim that Lee and I had actually connected and felt like we had taken a step closer to real friendship.

I walked into the condo, surprised by the sound of voices coming from the kitchen. "Hello?" My voice echoed down the hall.

"In here," Jim called. He was holding David and Lee was attempting to spoon avocado into his mouth. There was quite a bit on Jim's shirt and on the floor. David's cherubic little face was smeared green. It was a touching scene, and it felt like I was intruding in my own home.

"Lee, I thought you said you were going home?" My inquiry verged on confrontational.

"That was the plan, but I texted Jim when we were through and he suggested coming over here. It was so close to the dress shop, and taking the El with the stroller is a nightmare. Jim said he'd drive us back after the baby's nap."

It was a perfectly logical explanation, yet still I felt somehow excluded. My face must have betrayed my hesitation. Lee looked up at me and laughed. "Don't worry, I haven't told him a thing about your dress. My lips are sealed."

I willed myself to be friendly. "No worries. I don't

think Jim would understand the difference between a sweetheart bodice and halter top. His eyes would just glaze over and then he'd look at you and say, 'But it's white, right?'"

She and Jim laughed. "That sounds about right. Why don't I drive you guys over now? Abs, I'll see you later for dinner."

Lee finished cleaning up David and scooped him out of Jim's arms. "Thank you so much for inviting me, Abigail. I don't know when I've had so much fun. Your mother is a sweetheart. It was nice getting to know her."

After they had left, I went to change clothes before dinner, putting on some black pants and a simple top. I thought the outfit could use a little glamour, so I hunted through my jewelry box for a bracelet that had been a favorite of my grandmother. It was a dazzling, chunky gold bracelet from the 1960s.

A quick search through the box did not reveal the bracelet. I scoured through drawers, hoping it had fallen in, knocked off the dresser into a pile of clothes. I couldn't shake the feeling that someone had already rummaged through them. My crisply folded shirts had been wrinkled and everything was slightly askew. As a last resort, I was trying to shove the heavy dresser to see if it had fallen behind when the front door banged shut.

"Can you help me?" I called out to Jim. "I can't find my bracelet anywhere. You know the one from Nana? Maybe it fell behind here." He strode into the room, moved me out of the way, and gave the dresser a shove. "I don't see it. Do you think one of the maintenance guys might have stolen it? They're all so nice, it's hard to believe they would do such a thing, but I don't know who else it could be."

"When was the last time they were even in here?" He paused. "You know, maybe Lee took it. To borrow it, I mean. She was in here, with the baby. She yelled out about something but I couldn't really understand what she was saying. She must have asked if she could borrow it. Let me text her."

"Jim, that's totally not okay. Why wouldn't she have asked me when she saw me? I never would have said yes to that. That piece has a lot of sentimental value, not to mention, it's worth a fortune. She had no right to take it and it's pretty obvious she was rifling through my drawers. Everything is a mess."

"Don't be like that, Abby. She's family. I thought you guys bonded or whatever today. She probably just thought you'd be okay with it." He looked at me pleadingly. "Please don't make a big deal of it with her. I was so excited you guys were getting along. She means a lot to me."

Was I overreacting? The piece was large, she probably hadn't even thought it was gold, but some sort of cheap costume jewelry. It didn't explain why it looked as if she had gone through my underwear drawer, but to keep the peace, I would let it go. Jim was looking at me, waiting for my response.

"Fine, I won't say anything. Just get it back from her." Jim smiled, happy with my capitulation. "We'd better get going or we'll be late for our reservation."

****

As the wedding approached, Jim had given me his full attention. It was hard to tell which of us was more excited. Like the girl in my childhood fantasies spinning stories about prince charming, I was finally going to be a bride. Since the incident with the bracelet, I had not seen Lee. Jim still visited her and David regularly. She had sent me a text apologizing, saying she had not known the bracelet's value to me though she'd asked me about it years before. Taking the high road, I chose to think she'd simply forgotten.

A few weeks before the big day, our realtor called to tell us she had found the perfect house. It hadn't hit the MLS yet, but she thought it would go soon. It was being sold by a developer and he was expected to complete the house in the next month or two. We were excited to see it. It was near two train lines, just as Jim and I had joked about all those years ago. It was in Lakeview, sandwiched between the red and brown line, near the cute shops and restaurants of Southport. Lee was living on Southport herself, a few doors down from the brown line.

We saw the house and fell instantly in love. It was a five-bedroom house with room to spare for Jim's office and any kids we would have. The finishings were tasteful and elegant. The original exterior from the early 1900s had been restored. Inside, the developer had preserved a lot of the original woodwork while updating the common areas with chic new fixtures. We told our realtor to write up the contract and then walked over to Southport, jubilant, to grab dinner.

"This is wonderful, Abby. The house is gorgeous. It's only two blocks from Lee and both trains. I couldn't have asked for a better wedding gift. Do you love it?"

"I'm over the moon. It's amazing that we both agree on it. This house search was starting to make me despondent. It didn't seem like we'd ever find anything."

Jim's phone rang. "Lee! You're not going to believe it, dumpling! We're going to be neighbors. We found the perfect place. We're about to go get dinner and celebrate. Why don't you and David come meet us at that pasta place?" He paused while she responded. "Yeah, that's the one, the one you loved when we went there for your birthday."

I frowned. He rarely told me where they went when they went out. It was ridiculous that he had invited her to *our* celebration at her favorite restaurant, no less. When we arrived, she was already seated. Joining her, Jim began to list all the features of our new house. I turned away from them, babbling baby talk to David, half asleep in his stroller. Whatever attempts I made to join the conversation were rebuffed by their lukewarm replies. After dinner, Jim suggested we walk them home.

"Why don't you walk them home? I'm tired."

"It's two blocks, Abby. You're being ridiculous."

"Am I? You've literally not heard a thing I've said for the past hour. When the two of you are together, it's like I don't exist. You're marrying me in less than a month but you can't be bothered to pay any attention to me at a dinner that was supposed to be a celebration about our new home."

Jim looked at me stonily. "You know, why don't you go on home, then. Let's take some time apart for you to cool off. I'll spend the night on Lee's couch and see you in the morning." He stomped off grabbing Lee by the elbow.

I fought back tears. Crying in the middle of a

public street would be the crowning glory to my embarrassment. A Lethican did not lose control like that. Willing myself not to run after them, I stomped over to the train station and took the brown line home.

The next day was Sunday. Around noon, Jim came home. "Are you ready to apologize to me?"

"I think you owe me an apology as well. You were unbelievably rude through dinner."

"Abby, I will not apologize for entertaining Lee, who was our guest at dinner. You're being childish."

My nostrils flared and I inhaled deeply. This fight, which had started so small, had become the biggest one in our relationship. My frustration stemmed from his about face after our decision to buy the house, feeling so close to him compared with now, where he was acting like he was some sort of authority figure here to chastise me. Would arguing bring me the closeness I craved? It would only exacerbate the situation. "I'm sorry."

"Thank you. Now, if you don't mind, I have work to do." He pulled out his briefcase and began arranging papers on the dining room table. "What are you going to do with yourself today?"

Dismissed like a child, I reached for my purse and jacket. "I am going to drive up to see Mom and talk over last-minute wedding details." Jim didn't bother looking up, already too engrossed in his paperwork to acknowledge me.

****

"Oh, Mom, what is it about Lee that puts me so on edge?" I whined after rehashing last night's dinner over a cup of tea. "It feels like it's the two of them making me the intruder. It's nice that they are close and all, but she just seems to want him all to herself."

"Abby, you're being unkind. She's a single mother struggling to raise a child while working. You could have a bit more charity toward her."

"I have tried, Mom. You don't know what she's like."

"She was lovely while we were shopping for the dress, friendly and kind. And she dotes on that baby."

"I know. She was nice that day, but that was only the one day. And you know she stole my bracelet right after that."

"It was probably just a misunderstanding. She probably asked to borrow it and Jim just said yes, not really listening to the question. You know what men are like."

"You might be right, but what was she doing going through my stuff in the first place? Jim spends a lot of time with her when I'm traveling for work and more than once, things seemed to be out of place when I got home."

"Now you're just being paranoid, my dear. What do you propose? Do you want him to cut out the only family he has in Chicago from his life?" My mother paused, giving me a sharp look. "Do you want to cancel the wedding? Your father and I would understand. If you're having real doubts and not just last-minute jitters, we would support you."

My shoulders slumped into the chair. "No, Mom. Of course I don't want to cancel the wedding. And you're right. I'm probably making a mountain out of a molehill."

"Well, maybe now that you'll live so close to each other, you'll have more time to bond. She may not be your favorite person ever, but perhaps you can at least make peace with her."

"Thanks for listening, Mom." I gave her a hug. "You're right. I need to be more understanding and these are probably pre-wedding jitters. Getting married is starting to become very real."

"Don't be nervous. The hard part is all done. You just have to show up, look beautiful, and have the time of your life." She smiled and held me tight.

****

The morning of the wedding I woke up early, but in a fog. At the small rehearsal dinner, the champagne had been flowing liberally. Burying myself under the luxurious duvet, I looked around the large suite my family had booked for us at the Ritz. The opulent surroundings clashed with the banging going on in my head. The wedding was to be downstairs, in the ballroom. The women in my wedding party would come up here to get their hair and makeup done, in my enormous chambers. My mother had ordered lunch to be brought up while we were getting ready.

The rehearsal dinner had been fun, though clearly I was over served. Working my way through recollections of the night, a vision surfaced of Jim bringing me back here, then leaving to spend the night in our condo. Hopefully, I had not made too big of a fool of myself, but it was my wedding after all. I could get a little silly if I wanted to.

Going for a run would clear the cobwebs from my brain. My phone said it was forty degrees, decidedly balmy for January in Chicago. Sprinting down Michigan Avenue, I relished the solitude. The street was still clear of the shoppers that would crowd the pavement in a few hours. We would get ready and then take pictures at the venue before the guests arrived. My wedding day was finally here and it felt perfect already, sunny and clear.

Back at the hotel, I rinsed off, careful to keep my hair dry and sat like a queen wrapped in the hotel's thick cotton bathrobe, while the female members of my family started trickling in, cozy in joggers and sweatshirts, lugging their dresses and shoes. Lisa came in with her oldest daughter, Mae, now in eighth grade. Mae, being a teenager, had very specific opinions on how her makeup should be done and was fully engaged in pulling up pictures on her phone to show the stylist. My father's sister, my aunt Edith, followed closely behind, walking heavily on her cane. "Abby, my love! Last night was so much fun. I had too many glasses of wine and my rheumatism is not happy with me."

"Aunt Edith, sit down and rest. We're in no hurry. Where's Josie? Everything all right with the baby?" Edith's daughter, Josie, had just had her fourth child, a girl finally. The colicky baby had made a brief appearance the previous night before being rushed off crying by her exhausted parents.

"Everything's fine. She's just giving her one last feed before turning her over to Adam for a few hours. I'm glad she's getting a little break. Adam is a great father, but Josie never lets him get near that baby. It'll do her good to have a little separation, not to mention a little pampering."

"I let him near the baby, Mom. You're so dramatic. She's six weeks old. It's just easier for me to deal with her because she's still nursing all the time. Besides, this is my last baby. I want to remember every minute."

Josie approached and gave me a quick kiss on the cheek. "Speaking of remembering every minute, Abby, make sure you take time today to take little snapshots in your mind of your wedding. It goes by in a blur. You should have a minute, just the two of you after the ceremony to connect as husband and wife before you get mobbed by all the guests."

"What a lovely idea. I'll mention it to the wedding planner," my mother said, hearing the tail end of the conversation. A bellhop followed her in, rolling the luggage cart, her dress hanging in its protective sleeve, a professional grade steamer wedged underneath to take care of any wrinkles. My mother was always prepared for any eventuality.

Lisa started to get ready first. We sat around, snacking on the platters of food the kitchen had brought up, chatting about the night before. Lee was the last to arrive, pushing David in a stroller, the same bellhop now tripping over himself trying to help her while carrying in her dress. When she had settled herself, I stood up.

"It means so much to me that we're all here together today. This day is so special and you are all so special to me. I have some little gifts to show you how much I appreciate that you're all in my life." Lucy joined me walking back to the bedroom to get the packages.

"Can I help you carry anything?"

"Thanks, that would be great. It's mainly just trinkets. Actually, why don't I give you yours first?" I reached into the bag and pulled out a little Tiffany box. "I just want you to know how much our friendship has meant to me all these years, starting with when I was a scared freshman who would beg you to come shower with me because those communal bathrooms were so creepy."

"Ha, the whole dorm was creepy. You know they finally tore it down last year?"

"I'm not surprised. It was like a turn of the century insane asylum. I used to have a nightmare that someone was going to sneak by in the middle of the night and put bars on all the doors and lock us in. We had so much fun there, didn't we?"

"It's not over yet. We're still having fun. Just not as often. I've applied for a promotion that just came up in the Chicago office so hopefully we'll be together again soon."

"Really? That would be amazing. I have good friends here, but no one like you. You're the lone voice of reason in my life."

"Reason? Or do you mean sarcasm?"

"Maybe a little of both. Open it." I nudged the box at her.

"The earrings. The ones you let me borrow and then I lost them. I still feel terrible about that."

"Well, now you have your own pair. I hope you think of all the good times we had together whenever you wear them."

"I love them and I love you." She hugged me again, tears in her eyes. "I'm so happy for you, Abby, as long as you're sure he's the one."

"Yes, of course, I'm sure. Jim and I have been together so long at this point, I wouldn't know how to be without him. He's the right man for me."

"In that case, just make sure you throw the bouquet my way, okay?"

We gathered up the other gifts and went back to join the others. I presented each gift one at a time with a little story on why it had been chosen. For Lisa, I got an enamel ladybug brooch. While beautiful, it was really meant as a joke. At a family picnic when I was about three, I had gathered all the ladybugs I could find. When Lisa wasn't looking, I put them in her bowl of ice cream, hoping to surprise her. The ladybugs looked so beautiful decorating her pink strawberry ice cream. She took a bite without noticing, then gagged and ran away screaming when she realized the extra crunch in her dessert was bugs. My brothers had made fun of her for weeks. It had become part of the family lore. I was never trusted around anyone's ice cream again.

My aunt Edith collected antique thimbles. I had scoured the internet marketplaces, finally finding a silver Victorian era one, beautifully engraved with a nightingale. For Josie, I'd had a charm bracelet made, the first letter of each of her children's names swinging down, with a gift certificate for a massage and an offer to babysit tucked underneath.

Lee was the last on my list. She was sitting on the floor with David. I took out a little stuffy for David and gave Lee the box with the bracelet I had found for her.

"I was really excited to find this. You've always loved my grandmother's bracelet and it's almost an exact replica."

She smirked as she opened up the box. "Nothing but cheap imitations in my life. Ha." My body tensed up at her harsh words. "I'm just teasing. This is great. You're right. I have always admired that bracelet. It's beautiful."

I had waffled on buying it for her, worrying she

might consider it a passive aggressive scold for having borrowed the bracelet without asking. "I hope you'll wear it. If you don't want it though, there's a gift receipt. I didn't mean to dredge up any unpleasantness. It was meant as a bridge between us. I hope this wedding makes you think of me as family as well."

Her lips smiled thinly. "Sure, we'll all just be one big, happy family. Listen, you don't mind if I push the stroller into the bedroom and see if I can't get David to take a nap for a bit, do you?"

"Of course not." It was finally my turn to start getting glammed up and I went obediently to sit down in front of the hairstylist. My mother came over and took my hand.

"Oh, honey, you look so beautiful. Daddy and I are proud of you. When I was pregnant with you, don't get me wrong, I love your brothers, but I so desperately wanted a little girl. Then you came, and you were just everyone's favorite. You're still just a little girl in my mind. It means so much to me to get to see you walk down the aisle, and build a life with Jim, but it's hard to think of you as a grown-up. I love you, darling." She leaned in and kissed me. We were both tearing up.

Lisa came over. "I'm all for the heartfelt gestures, but you two need to keep your makeup streak free until at least after the ceremony." She had pinned her brooch on her dress. "By the way, I love this. It's beautiful."

"I'm so glad. You know you're like a big sister to me."

"Well, your big sister here says we need to get this show on the road soon. It's time to put on your dress and head downstairs for pictures."

My mother nodded. "You don't want to keep Jim

waiting." We finished getting ready and headed down to the venue.

After taking some family pictures, Linda, the wedding planner, directed us to queue up for the ceremony. Jim, debonair in his custom tuxedo, went ahead to stand at the head of the aisle, under a bower of hanging roses with crystals threaded through. My father ushered me into a little room where we would remain hidden until the guests arrived.

"How are you feeling about everything, my little nightingale? Nervous?"

"A little. I'll be relieved once it's over. This dress is so long. I don't want to trip and make a fool of myself."

"Don't worry. We'll go slow and you'll have my arm to steady you. I love you, my sweet daughter. Jim is a good, upstanding man. You chose well. Enjoy yourself today and always remember to take time for each other every day in your marriage, no matter how busy the two of you get."

"Oh, Daddy. I can only hope we're as happy as you and Mom. You two are awe-inspiring."

Linda bobbed her head through the doorway. "It's go time."

My dad winged his elbow at me and we started walking slowly, with me counting to keep the pace as the planner had instructed during the rehearsal. The rest of the ceremony was a daze as I kept my eyes locked with Jim's standing before the altar. The priest's booming voice cut through with the ultimate question and I gave my assent, loud and clear. Jim said his "I do" and then it was over, with my new husband pulling me in for a kiss before our dearest family and friends. We flew down the aisle amid clapping and cheering, my brothers whooping it up like they were at a football game. When we reached the exit, Linda was there with champagne.

"I've set up a little table for the two of you with some appetizers to give you a minute alone while the guests shift to the cocktail reception. Take your time, savor it, and when you're ready, you can join them."

"In here?" When Linda nodded, Jim looked at me and said, "Hold on tight now." He reached around my voluminous dress and swept me up into his arms.

"Jim!! What are you doing? You're supposed to carry me over the threshold of our house, not at the wedding."

"I'm practicing. Can't a man hold his wife when he damn well feels like it?"

I laughed, giddy, as he carried me into the room. Kicking the door closed, he sat on the couch, with me in his lap. "Now, I also think a man should be able to kiss his wife when he feels like it. Any objections to that one, Mrs. Hardy?"

"Oh no, Mr. Hardy, I would never contradict my husband on such an important point." The next few minutes we explored each other's lips, somehow more special now that were married.

I was the first to break away. "We should eat something. We're supposed to make the rounds to each of the tables once dinner starts."

"Yes, ma'am." He popped a large shrimp into his mouth. "Thank you for being in my life, Abby. I'm not always the most affectionate person, especially when work gets hectic, but know that I appreciate you always. You mean the world to me, my darling, and you've made me the happiest of men by becoming my wife. Also, that dress looks damn good on you."

"Why thank you." I gave a little twirl as the planner came back to lead us into the cocktail reception. The rest of the evening passed in a blur of family and friends, good food and dancing, with Jim by my side. My happiness felt complete. My mother was right. With so much love in my life, I could spare a little empathy for Lee.

Chapter 7

A few weeks after moving into our new house, I came home from work to find a large box on the stoop. "Arg!" My frustration rose. The mattress for the guest room had arrived, one of those latex ones that expand miraculously when you open the box. Initially, it had seemed better than dealing with meeting a delivery company and taking a day off work. Unfortunately, the thing had arrived at the same time as a text from Jim saying he wouldn't be home before midnight. Getting the hundred pound box up the stoop into the house before the rain started would be a challenge, let alone to the second floor.

I propped the front door open. Using my full weight against it, I could hopefully shove it up the few short steps into the house.

"Do you want some help?" a deep voice said close behind me. I jumped, nearly tripping over the box in front of me.

"Oh my God, you scared me." I found myself looking into a pair of very green eyes with an undertone of blue.

"I'm Jake, from next door." He gave me his outstretched hand. Tall and wiry, this man was about Jim's height, but without the broadness of shoulder. His dark hair was haphazardly tied up in one of those man buns so popular with the young college bros in the neighborhood, with sparse facial hair making up a fledgling beard. He wore a torn Pink Floyd shirt. The lines around his eyes that crinkled with his smile were at odds with his youthful attire. "I promise I'm not some psychopath. Scout's honor," he said, holding up two fingers.

The hand before me was calloused and stained. "Were you actually ever a scout?" My words unintentionally came off with a flirtatious undertone.

"Er, actually, no. Is that going to be a problem?" His grin spread wider.

"No, sorry, I was just being…silly. I'm Abigail and I would love some help."

He looked at the box, pointing to handles that had been carved in at the top. "You take one end, and I'll take the other." Together, we managed to wiggle it up the stairs. Just then, a loud crack of thunder exploded and the heavens opened up. "As always, perfect timing on my part," Jake said. "Well, is this going upstairs? It might be easier if we take it out of the box."

"You don't have to do that. My husband will be home later, he can help me get it up the stairs." Silently, I thought the box had a high chance of sitting in the entryway for days before Jim could be troubled to take it upstairs.

"Really, it's no trouble. Besides, leaving now would guarantee I was drenched before I crossed the ten steps next door."

Hesitation furrowed across my brow. Jake stood there, his eyebrow quirked expectantly. What was I doing with this total stranger in my house? Jim would most definitely not approve, but really, the guy was just being neighborly.

"Okay, let me get a knife from the kitchen."

"No need. I have one in my pocket." Reaching in, he pulled out a large folding knife, the kind a hunter might have, and started sawing away. He winked at the surprised expression on my face. "Trust me, it's a handy thing to have."

Extricating the mattress, we each grabbed a side and started up the stairs. "How do you like the neighborhood so far?"

"It's cute," I tried to say without grunting. "I love the restaurants and shops on Southport, and it's so nice being only two blocks from the El stop, but the Cubs traffic is a little exhausting. We used to live downtown. It's a nice change having a house with a yard and not living my life riding up and down in an elevator every time I want to go outside."

"Makes sense. I actually grew up here. Without Cubs traffic, my life would lose all its meaning." His teasing smile came back.

"This neighborhood must be so different from when you were a kid."

"Oh, yeah, much more gentrified. This area was a blue-collar spot when I was little, a little rough around the edges, just like me." He winked at me again.

At the top of the stairs, we stopped. "Well, obviously, the bedroom in question is all the way down the hall."

"Of course it is. I can probably get it there myself if you'll just lead the way."

With so many siblings, I struggled with silence. Walking down the hall, my prattling continued. "We don't have kids yet so we haven't done anything to these rooms. I'll just leave them empty until the time comes."

"It's a big house. How many kids are you planning on?"

Something in the way he looked at me made me blush, as if he were picturing the very act that would result in so many offspring. "Well, I'm the youngest of four, so I have always wanted a big family. I take it you don't have kids yet?"

"Nope, haven't found the right lady yet. I was an only child, though. It would have been nice to have grown up in a big family, assuming you all like each other, of course."

"We were all close for the most part, though they drove me crazy. I was the only girl."

Once in the bedroom, Jake began cutting open the bag. "It's going to unfold and pop a bit, then we can put it on to the bed frame."

Reaching out to help open the bag, I lost my footing. Jake reached out and grabbed me. "Whoa, easy. You okay?"

"I must have slipped on the plastic." His hands remained tight on my shoulders as I gazed up, getting my bearings. His lashes were long and gave his face an almost feminine quality, so at odds with the sinewiness of his hands.

"You smell nice," he said simply, looking into my face.

Turning away, I blurted out, "That might not be an appropriate comment from a neighbor, Jake." His own smell lingered in my nostrils, a combination of sweat, old spice, and something I couldn't quite put my finger on.

"Fine, I retract the statement." His hands went

down to his sides. "You actually smell putrid. Most foul, even."

My lips quirked in amusement. "Ha. Thanks…that might be going too far in the other direction."

"Ah, women, you are all so fickle, you never know what you want."

I shook my head playfully. Jake was refreshingly funny, and not quite the frat boy I had first assumed.

His phone dinged. He pulled it out of his pocket. "Arg, not again. One of my tenants is having issues with his toilet again. I seriously think he puts bowling balls in there. I have to go but let me help you get this on the frame first."

"Seriously, if you have to go, don't worry about it."

"Yeah, they can wait a few minutes. Maybe if I make them wait a few hours, they will learn their lesson."

We grabbed either side of the mattress and heaved. "Do you want me to take the box out to the alley?"

"No, I can handle it. You've been more than helpful. I don't know how to thank you."

"No problem, just being neighborly." He turned toward the door, and then turned again. "Listen, I'm having a little barbeque this Saturday in the backyard if you're free. There will even be beer pong."

"Oh wow, beer pong, huh? It's been a long time since I've done that." In reality, I had never been the kind of girl to play beer pong. "Maybe, but let me check with my husband first."

"Cool, I'll let myself out."

After he left, it took my nerves a while to settle, as if I'd been caught in some indiscretion. I shook off the feeling and went looking for some sheets.

****

When Jim came home, I was already sound asleep. The movement of the mattress woke me and I reached my arm over to embrace him. "Hey," he said, kissing my forehead. "How was your day? Work okay?"

"Sure, fine." The comforter muffled my sleepy reply.

"What's that big empty box downstairs?"

"The mattress for the guest room came in. I didn't want to take the box out in the rain so I left it in the kitchen until tomorrow."

"No worries, I can do it. Where's the mattress? You didn't carry it by yourself?"

"No, our neighbor, Jake, saw me struggling and helped me carry it in."

"You let a total stranger into our house? Abby, that's dangerous."

"He's just a nice guy who offered to help, not a rapist or a burglar."

"You're too trusting, Abigail. I know the world you grew up in. People in your town never lock their doors, but in the real world, you have to be cautious." He pulled his arm away. "I'm tired. Can we talk about this tomorrow?"

"There's nothing to talk about. He's just a nice guy who has also invited us over for a barbeque next Saturday. You can see for yourself."

"Good night, Abigail." Jim rolled away from me and my eyes remained glued to the ceiling, wishing I hadn't woken up. Still stinging from being lectured, the minutes stretched out but sleep did not come.

My alarm was set to 5:30 and I rushed to silence it

so Jim could sleep later. Our schedules were very different, with Jim getting up long after my day had begun and coming home after I'd gone to sleep. It felt like we were roommates, though this was supposed to be a temporary situation. Jim had to put in the effort to make partner at the law firm. Maybe then he could slow down and we could begin our family. Buying this house and moving to a more kid friendly neighborhood had been a start in the right direction but, so far, the baby hadn't materialized. With the infrequent nature of our sex life, it was hardly a surprise. My suggestion of talking to a fertility specialist had been rebuffed. Jim's response was to tell me he didn't have that kind of time right now. Without the time to make a baby, it was improbable that he'd have time day to day to parent one once it had arrived, but that was a burden I was willing to bear on my own. It felt pathetic, begging him to make love to me when it was "the right time". With fertility treatments, I could at least retain my pride. In the past month, we hadn't even tried. He was never home, and seemed so uninterested in sex. Really, he didn't even seem interested in talking to me.

****

Saturday morning, I woke early to go to spin class, and let Jim sleep in. After an endorphin boost from a good workout, my resolve strengthened to try harder to bridge the gap permeating my life with my husband. I stopped for bagels and coffee from Jim's favorite deli, ambling home down the sidewalk next to our house. Chicago houses are set close together, separated by gangways, but they offer privacy. The windows on one house never line up with the house next to it. The bay of our dining room, for example, had two windows on either side, with a wall in between, so you could see down the gangway, but not into the other house. The neighboring house, in turn, had a large window facing the brick wall portion of the bay. All the houses on the block were raised, with ample sized windows for the basement.

Stepping out of the narrow gangway into the yard, the warm sun hit my face. I lingered in the perfect morning and stretched out my tight leg muscles on the back of a chair on the small patio. The birds lulled me with their sweet song. I rotated my torso to stretch my hip and was startled by Jake, standing on his neighboring porch, staring at me.

"Hey, sorry, didn't mean to startle you." Jake's embarrassment was clear on his face.

"How long have you been standing there?" Glancing downward, I was concerned my sweat drenched clothes were now verging on see through.

"Long enough to be concerned you had fallen into some sort of cosmic yogi meditation and were going to start chanting. You're really flexible." His green eyes lit up with the innuendo.

"Funny. I was just trying to stretch out a little. Must have zoned out."

"Your coffee is probably cold by now. I just put on a full pot if you need a refill." His arm motioned behind him to what was presumably the kitchen.

"That's really nice of you. I don't mind cold coffee, though." Stupidly, my mind reached for another topic to keep the conversation going. "Are you getting ready for your party?"

"Yeah, I was about to set up some tables. Are you going to come?"

"Definitely." There was an awkward pause as we locked glances over the fence. "Well, I'd better head in and give Jim his bagel while it's still fresh."

"Don't indulge too much this morning. Party will start around two and I make a mean hamburger."

"Oh really, we'll see about that. I happen to be a hamburger connoisseur. It's been weighing on me, though—is it required that I play beer pong?"

"Ha, only if you're terrible. Then you have to play against me." His evenly tanned skin creased easily into smile lines as he started down the steps of his porch. "Also, no need to come around—there's a secret panel in the fence." His voice boomed from behind the six foot tall privacy fence between our two yards, their identical footprint in parallel. A smooth metallic sound pinged and the panel slid over.

"Wow, that's crazy. I had no idea it was there. Why would the developer leave it?"

"Technically, this is my fence, so he had no right to change it, but yeah, I doubt he knew about it. My grandfather owned both the buildings. He put it in so I could go between without having to go out to the street. We lived on the second floor of this one and my grandfather on the first. When my mom started her own hair salon, he let her do it in the basement of what is now your house. We had a little compound."

"That's really cool."

"Well, you're welcome to use it anytime you need to borrow a cup of sugar, neighbor." I studied his rugged face. While not classically handsome, there was an irresistible kindness about him. His long lashes remained still as we stood there a beat too long in silence, eyes locked.

The screen door behind me clanked open. "Abby, you coming in with that coffee? It's going to get cold."

"Coming, Jim, just getting the details on the barbeque this afternoon." I smiled back at Jake, the politician's daughter's smile on my face. "Thank you so much for showing me the door. It's very well done. We'll be sure to stop by this afternoon." I turned, breathing deeply, and headed into the house with the errant coffees, wondering what it was about my neighbor that fascinated me. He was so unlike the white collar, North Shore types with whom I had grown up. The fake smile remained plastered on my face. "I'm so sorry about the coffee, Jim. Hopefully, you had a good rest."

"Abby, I don't like the way he looks at you. It's not appropriate."

Was it possible the great and desirable Jim Hardy was jealous? While irrational, the thought pleased me. "You can't possibly think he's interested in me."

Jim's gaze traveled slowly over me, from head to toe. "You're probably right. He probably hates the gentrification that is happening in this neighborhood and is trying to get my goat."

My bubble properly deflated, the snippiness threaded through my response. "Maybe he's just curious about us. His grandfather used to own this when it was a two flat. Jake is the one who sold it to the developer. Gentrification has likely done wonders for his bank account. The party starts at two. We really should stop by, at least for a bit."

"For a bit, since apparently you already agreed to it. Don't forget, we are bringing dinner over to Lee and David."

"I haven't forgotten. The ingredients are in the fridge. I'm going to put together a pasta bake and just pop it in the oven over there. If you guys want to go out and grab a drink afterwards and catch up, I don't mind staying with David. She could probably use some time out of the house."

"She has been feeling a little stir crazy. The little guy is teething and has been a handful. Thank you for the suggestion." He winked at me. "That's a nice idea, Abigail."

I smiled, happy at both the praise and the shift away from our discussion about the neighbor. "Glad to help."

The rest of my morning was spent cooking. Jim continued to work in the dining room. Through the kitchen window, I watched Jake setting up the small yard. Distracted, my hand knocked the pan off the counter. Jim snapped at me to keep it down. What was the point of buying this big house if he was just going to spread out over the dining room again, instead of taking the time to set up his office? Was this how marriages failed, through a series of small resentments building up over time, with no reprieve?

Two o'clock had come and gone. We were due at Lee's house at five. Approaching Jim, I steeled myself and asked, "Will you be finished soon? We really should stop by the barbeque, and it's almost time to leave for dinner."

"Well, you're the one who said we were going, without even asking me. Quite frankly, I have no interest in socializing with those people."

"Fine. You can stay home."

My anger propelled me through the door as Jim

called at my back. "Abby, don't you dare!"

Once in the bright sunlight, I stopped to look over at the neighboring yard, full of people laughing, the music turned up. A waft of smoke curled up from the barbeque. The sound of the screen door snapping shut behind me caught Jake's attention. "Coming over?" His smile was wide and welcoming.

"Yes! Can you open the secret door for me?"

I rushed down into the yard before Jim decided to follow me out and make a scene. Jake took me around, introducing me to his friends. Most of the people were congregating by the make shift ping-pong table, the red solo cups filled to the brim with beer. This was so different than the socializing in my life. Everyone seemed to be having fun, the laughter echoing between friends. "Are you ready for that burger?"

"I am, thanks." Near the grill, a station of buns and condiments had been set up. There was a tray of cooked burgers, and Jake began to put one together for me. I took it from him and bit into it. "Wow. This is actually a great burger."

"I should take the compliment, but your tone is a little insulting. You thought I would fall short of the mark."

"You're right, I'm surprised. Keeping up the quality when cooking for this many people is a real skill."

"It's all about keeping the patties evenly sized. If you measure them all out beforehand, they'll cook evenly."

"You spend a lot of time thinking about this." My voice was light and teasing.

"Any man worth his salt spends a lot of time

thinking about meat and what he can do to make it taste even better. Honestly, once summer grilling season starts, it's a wonder anyone even shows up to work. And don't get me started on smoking meat. We'd be here for days."

Distracted, I had not noticed Jim appear behind me. "Hi! Did you finish up your work?"

"For now." He eyed Jake warily. "You must be Jake. I'm Jim." They shook hands. "Thanks for inviting us over and helping Abby with the mattress the other day. Those burgers smell good. Mind if I grab one?"

"Of course, man. Be my guest. Let me go grab you a beer too." He strode off to the cooler on the opposite end of the yard.

Jim scowled at me while smearing ketchup on his burger. "So you snuck over here to flirt with the neighbor? You know I didn't want to go to this damn barbeque. What exactly are you trying to prove?"

"I'm not trying to prove anything. It would be nice to make friends with the neighbors. That's all."

"With these people," he muttered under his breath, looking around at Jim's friends, casual in cargo shorts, chugging cheap beer on their Saturday. "These people hardly warrant our time, Abby. You should know better."

"They are people and they are kind. I was enjoying myself until you showed up."

"Flirting like a schoolgirl with that bearded hippie. You should be ashamed of yourself. You look ridiculous."

Jake crossed back to us with the beer and handed it to Jim. "You want me to introduce you around?"

Biting back tears, I took a deep breath. "We have a

dinner engagement and need to get going."

Jim nodded at the burger in his hand. "Thanks again, man. Mind if I take this back to our place while she gets ready? You know women, they take forever to put on their face or whatever it is they do."

"Yeah, no worries. Thanks for stopping by. I'll see you guys around."

We walked back through the secret gate. I stomped up the stairs and ran to our room, locking the door. Tears of humiliation streamed down my face. Jim would never follow me. I would stay in our room until it was time to go and then he would act like nothing happened, or worse yet, expect me to apologize. Marriage was about compromise, but it felt like I was the only one in this relationship who understood that.

Chapter 8

A few days later, I stopped off after work to pick up a sandwich before heading back to my empty home. It was a beautiful evening. It would be a treat to take off my shoes, put on some comfy shorts, eat dinner on the back porch and listen to my favorite podcast. I opened the back door, expecting the sound of birds and children playing down the street. My ears were instead assaulted by a TV announcer barking out the play-by-play of the baseball game being played a few blocks away at Wrigley Field. Jake was lounging on his porch, live streaming the game on his laptop.

"Wouldn't you be more comfortable watching it on the big screen in your house? Or possibly walking over there and getting some cheap last-minute seats?" I called over, somewhat teasingly, hiding my annoyance that my plans had been disrupted.

"I do like going to the game, but it's been a long day. Watch it from inside though? Absolutely not. Only if it's an away game. Otherwise, the fans cheering is like surround sound. If the wind is just right, you can even hear them singing Take Me Out to the Ball Game in the seventh inning. It's like you're actually there."

I stared at him, amused. "You're quite the baseball enthusiast."

"The Cubs are my team. I grew up three blocks from the ballpark. It's like a religion around here. Let me guess, you know nothing about baseball."

"With three brothers? I can't help knowing a little about baseball. Don't let me ruin the experience. With my headphones on, you won't even know I'm here."

"I don't mind. In fact, you're welcome to come sit with me. Maybe you would enjoy a little refresher course on what's been happening in baseball land... unless Jim is inside waiting for you."

Expectation filled the space between us. I was embarrassed to admit it but Jim would likely leave the office long after the game had ended. I respected his need to work but felt the heartache of never being a priority. At least this evening would not be another one spent on my own. "Sure, mind if I bring over my sandwich? I still haven't eaten."

"Come over. There's leftover pizza in the fridge, if you're interested. Can I get you a beer? Baseball and beer kind of go together."

Laughing, I made my way down the steps to the secret gate and found the latch with ease. "You know, why not? Just one, though."

He went into the kitchen to get me a plate and the beer as I settled into the porch swing, eyeing its beauty. The intricate carving would have been fit for an Indian palace and was at odds with Jake's college bro persona.

"This is gorgeous," I gushed as he came back out, my hands resting lightly on the armrest. "Where ever did you get this from? I've never seen anything like it."

"Do you like it?" His expression was earnest, devoid of his usual jocularity. "It's my own design. That's actually what I do. I own the furniture store over on Southport and make custom wood pieces for an exorbitant amount of money."

"You made this? That's amazing. How long have you been doing this?" I thought back to when he had helped me with the mattress. That smell of chemicals and sweat I had found so masculine had been the smell of wood stain.

"I've had the shop for about five years. My grandfather taught me woodworking initially. It became a passion of mine. After his passing, his will named me his sole beneficiary, with a letter encouraging me to follow my dreams. He left behind a small fortune, if I can say that without being rude. There were quite a few buildings in his real estate portfolio, most of them mortgage free and printing money. I sold off the ones that developers wanted for single-family homes, like yours, and kept a few of the larger multi-unit ones. My grandfather had lived so simply, it all came as a surprise. Which seems absolutely ridiculous, considering in my previous life I had been an accountant."

My eyes widened. The man beside me did not fit with the image of a straight-laced accountant in a button down and crew cut, pouring over spreadsheets. "No kidding. What a story. How long were you an accountant?"

"Only three years. But enough about me. What about you and the lord of the manor over there? Let me guess. He comes from a rich southern family and just swept you off your feet, showering you with gifts."

"Oh no, you have Jim all wrong. We met in college at Vanderbilt. He's a brilliant small-town boy from Tennessee who got there on a basketball scholarship. He may come off as cold but there is a lot of stress that goes along with all his ambition."

"And do you hail from the south?"

"No, Winnetka actually. I had a very lovely childhood, loving family, summers either at the lake house or away at camp...the quintessential suburban existence."

"Sounds a little bougie. Let me guess, daddy is a lawyer and your mother stayed home and played tennis at the country club."

A blush crept up my face. "You're close to the truth, but my mom did more than just play tennis. Also, there were four children, it's not like she had a ton of free time."

"Does your dad still practice?"

"Ah, no, he's moved onto government work." I faltered, not wanting to mention my father was our senator. It was so nice to have a conversation with someone who did not know about my family, that was not impressed with me because of my family. "Anyway, how many pieces do you sell a month? It must be pretty labor intensive work."

"It is, but there are a couple of guys I trained working alongside me. Depends on the piece, of course, but we usually get through about five a month. I try not to turn people away, but if they have a tight timeline, I won't work with them. I want each piece to the get the attention it deserves." The pride rang in his voice. "If there's anything you need for the house, I'd love to make it, giving you the good neighbor discount, of course." His body was close, the swing no bigger than a loveseat. His green eyes locked with mine for a moment before they traveled down to my lips, causing me to nervously lick them. For a second, I thought he was going to kiss me and I jumped up, panicked.

"That is a tempting offer. We really need a new dresser for the master. The space is much larger than our old place and I'd like something bigger. Jim should be home soon. I really should go see about finding him some dinner. Thanks so much for the beer, though you definitely failed in your duties to teach me more about baseball." I smiled, grabbing my plate, intending to take it into the kitchen.

His fingers brushed mine as he reached for it. My heart thumped. "Don't worry about it. Thanks for stopping by. You know there are a lot of baseball games in the summer, so I'll be right here, ready to tutor you when you have some free time."

"Sounds like a plan." I hurried across the yard and back to the safety of my own house.

Once inside, frustration and shame overcame me. Was I, a newly married woman, so desperate for attention that a simple smile and a little conversation had me giddy like a schoolgirl? Jim was at work, building a career that would benefit both of us, not gallivanting about town. I resolved I would not avoid Jake but would try to establish myself as his friend only. It was probably foolish of me to think Jake even found me attractive. There had been a dozen women flirting with him at his barbeque, all of them pretty. He'd hardly have his head turned by a plain Jane like me, a married one no less.

****

As the weeks of summer went by, Jim continued to work long hours, even on the weekends, though we usually had dinner Sunday nights with Lee and David. Jim had always made room in his schedule for David. Jake and I settled into an easy friendship and the thought that there had ever been any sexual tension between us seemed silly. On occasion, we watched baseball games together, Jake teaching me the names of the players and the stats of the different teams. It eased my loneliness. House hunting had taken up so much time that once the project was over, my life felt a little empty. It was nice to have someone to come home to, even if it was just a neighbor. Jim didn't know I had been spending so much time with Jake. When we took Lee and David to a game one Sunday, his surprise at my baseball acumen was clear.

"Abby, you take everything so seriously. We move to Wrigleyville, and you have to become an expert on the Cubs. It's a nice quality." His smile glowed as he took my hand. I blushed, embarrassed that this newfound knowledge had come from spending time with another man. Conflicted, I regretted keeping our visits a secret. After so many years together, it was nice to have this hidden little world be all my own. When Jim was working his attitude was distant, rarely speaking of his colleagues, or even the cases he had been working on, answering any interest on my part with a simple, "I think about work enough at the office, Abby."

With Jake, we were comfortable in each other's company, though the friendship had taken on a casual, almost impersonal bent. Since the first night, we hadn't spoken of our families, or my marriage, just baseball, his business, or my day at work. The visits were at most once a week, but I'd begun to look forward to those evenings. Perhaps that was wrong. As summer stretched into fall, and the season ended, we would not have our evenings on the porch much longer, though likely it was for the best.

Lee looked over at me from the other side of Jim. It seemed like Lee always had Jim between us, our friendship not quite complete when we were alone. Still, the arrangement had become an amicable one. I loved David, he was a darling little boy, but Lee and I rarely had anything to say to each other that didn't relate to the child. Sometimes I wondered if her evenings were as lonely as mine, coming home from work with only a toddler for company. Her life was a mystery. Her dating life was a secret, though as a single mom it must have been difficult to juggle finding the time. Her curves had snapped right back after childbirth and any man would find her attractive.

"Lee, I'm heading to the ladies' room. Do you want to go together? You could probably use an extra pair of hands changing diapers."

"Sure, that would be great. Do you mind carrying the diaper bag?"

As we headed up the stairs, away from our seats, I turned to her. "Listen, Lee, I don't know if you're dating or anything, but I'm always happy to watch David one night a week if you want to go out and grab a drink or dinner. It's got to be hard trying to schedule dates with kids."

Her cat shaped eyes glanced at me sideways. "Dating has not been at the forefront of my thoughts. It's funny, just this week, Jim also thought maybe I should start thinking about finding someone now that David is getting older."

Bitterness turned her voice hard. Perhaps she had been nursing a hope of getting back together with the father and Jim had suggested she move on? With me, the topic of David's father had been strictly off limits since our discussion of the birth certificate.

At the top of the narrow stairs, the man next to me gave me a sharp shove.

"Hey! Watch it!" I looked over. "Devin, seriously? I could have fallen and knocked down Lee and the baby."

He smirked and shook his head. "Easy, Abby, you're such a drama queen, yet again." Peering over me, his mouth spread into a friendly grin as he looked at Lee. "Hey, neighbor. I didn't know you were coming out to the game today."

"Wait, you guys are neighbors? When did you move?"

"Yeah, my lease was up. I wanted to be closer to the train. This promotion has me starting earlier in the morning, so the shorter commute is great." Since my father threatened to cut him off years ago, Devin had taken a job in marketing and ad sales and was, by all accounts, actually thriving. It was hard for me to imagine him being charming enough to sell anyone anything, but I admit my bias.

Lee smiled, her dimples on display. "He moved in last week, right across the hall from me."

"Now whenever you need a pickle jar opened, you just have to knock." Devin winked flirtatiously. My eyes ping-ponged between them, surprised at the sexual charge in the air. Was Lee actually interested in my brother, or was this just her flirtatious default mode? David started squirming in his mother's arms. "Here, let me take him. Where you guys headed? I can put him up on my shoulders so he can get a bird's-eye view. Would you like that, little man?"

My shock was complete as I saw my idiot brother reach for the child, swoop him up and place him on his shoulders. David giggled with glee. "So high!"

"We're headed to the ladies room." I stepped in front, allowing them some privacy. Though my instinct was to be disturbed by this development, it wasn't a total surprise. They had met on and off through the years at various gatherings, and my brother was not unattractive. If she'd fallen for a married jerk, falling for an unmarried jerk this time was an improvement. Plus, my brother's reputation with women was not terrible. There had been a few girlfriends through the years, all of the breakups amicable. He seemed to treat other, non-sibling women well, actually. I smiled, excited to share this little detail with Jim later.

After the Cubs game, while walking home, David fell asleep in Jim's arms. The mood around us was jubilant. The Cubs had made the playoffs. Jim and Lee chatted happily. Walking slightly behind them on the crowded sidewalk, I studied them, struck by how natural they seemed together, two beautiful people, holding a beautiful little boy. A pang of jealousy surged within me, though I knew that was ridiculous. I rarely ever thought about the disparity between my looks and Jim's anymore, but seeing two such perfect specimens next to each other was like walking into a Calvin Klein commercial. David snuggled tighter in his perch and Jim gave his little head of curls a gentle kiss. We turned down Southport toward Lee's building. A panting voice behind me shouted, "Hold up."

Turning back, we saw Devin sprinting his way through the crowds. "Ugh, beer and running do not mix. Is it okay if I walk back with you guys? I can take a turn with him if he's getting heavy, Jim."

Jim looked at him, anger bubbling beneath the surface. After Jim's initial contentious meeting with Devin, they'd never attempted to become friends, keeping their relationship on the cool side of cordial. "He's not heavy. We don't want to keep you from your day."

"No worries. I have no plans, just heading home." Devin smiled at Lee with puppy dog eyes as he said the word "home". It was increasingly unclear if they had gone past the flirting stage.

I looked at Jim. "It turns out Devin has moved across the hall from Lee, so they're neighbors now."

Jim's face grew stormier still. Lee smiled and looked pointedly at Jim. "Really, Jim, there's no reason for you to walk the extra blocks to my place. Devin can walk me home." Her seductive gaze settled on Devin and I watched my brother preen under the attention.

Worried Jim was about to explode, I was going to speak up to diffuse the situation when Jake popped out of the store next to us. "Hey, guys, was that game amazing or what?"

"You must be so excited. That was pretty great." The surprise of seeing Jake brought a wave of happiness over me. His smile was magnetic.

"Abby, we're going to have to do something special for the first playoff game. Maybe we'll order lobster or something ridiculous for dinner that night."

My expression froze. Jim looked at me and said, "Why would you two be ordering dinner together?"

I looked at Jake, willing him quiet. "You're definitely going to want to be at that first game in person. Is this your store?"

Jake looked at me speculatively for a moment, as my cheeks flushed. He was clearly registering that I hadn't mentioned ordering takeout together, keeping the extent of our friendship a secret from my husband. "It is. Would you guys like to come and take a look? I'm actually working on a dresser right now, similar to the one you were thinking about getting for your place. I could customize it to fit the space." He looked over at Lee and Devin. "I'm Jake, by the way."

"Oh my goodness, I'm so sorry. This is Lee, Jim's cousin, and her son David. This oversized child is actually my brother Devin." On cue, Devin stuck out his tongue. "Jake is our neighbor."

"Nice to meet you, man," said Devin, shaking hands. He looked at Jim. "You guys should take a look. I've been in your shop, Jake, and the pieces are amazing. Here, I'll take David and head back with Lee." His arms reached toward the sleeping child.

"Oh thanks, Devin. Well, we'll see you guys later," Lee pronounced, looking forcefully at Jim, who looked down at David, realizing he would have to hand him over or make a scene.

They turned away and I smiled at Jake, unnerved by the awkwardness of the moment. "Let's see what you have."

The pieces in the store were mesmerizing. They evoked old world charm with a modern edge. The level of care and attention and detail Jake had poured into his work was astounding. I looked up over at Jim to see if he was impressed. He was taking a cursory look at the pieces while checking his email on the other side of the store. Jake stood near me, waiting for my response, his intense expression nervous. I swallowed, uncertain.

"This is amazing, Jake. Truly. You have a gift."

Relief warmed his features. "I'm glad you think so. Your opinion means a lot to me." He looked down at his hands. "The lobster comment was a mistake. I assumed you would have told him that we hang out sometimes."

"Yeah, I should have but it never seemed important." My lame response landed flat between us.

His stained hands fidgeted with a pen. "Right. The piece is in the back."

He turned to walk away, hurt by my insensitive comment. "I'm sorry."

"No biggie. Hey, Jim," he called. "The piece is over here if you want to see it."

The two men looked over the dresser, discussing price and delivery times. Jim told him he'd think about it. Wishing we'd never come inside, I interrupted. "We should really get going or we'll be late for dinner."

"You're right. I have to write up something for work real quick. We should be going." He looked at Jake and said, "Thanks again. You going out tonight to celebrate the Cubs? The neighborhood is going to be wild."

"No actually, I have a date tonight. You guys enjoy your evening. Let me know on the piece. I can come by and measure whenever."

Jim's mood was sullen as we walked home.

"Today was a lot of fun. It was so sweet seeing David at his first game," I said, looking over at him hopefully, trying to steer the conversation, knowing how much he cared for Lee's son.

"Yeah, I'm glad we went. He was pretty well behaved. Maybe we could try taking him to a basketball

116

game in the winter."

"Aren't those usually night games? I think that's probably past his bedtime."

"Yeah, I guess you're right." He settled back into silence.

"Listen, about Jake."

"What about him? I can't believe that guy actually has talent. The furniture was beautiful, though crazy expensive. What was the lobster comment about? A thank you for spending so much money?"

"No, it's just, a couple of times he's invited me over to watch the Cubs game with him when he has extra pizza. We just sit on the porch and watch. No big. It was just a joke."

Jim looked at me curiously. "You guys hang out that much? You shouldn't be that friendly with him."

"It was a couple of times over the summer. I won't even see him now that it's getting cold out."

"Whatever you think."

"Are you mad?"

"What, about that guy? No. Listen, Abby. You need to tell your brother to stay away from Lee. He's no good. I don't want him bothering her."

"Lee. Right." I paused, surprised he was still thinking about them.

"It's not good for David to have strange men around. Devin is not serious about her. You've said it yourself—he's just an overgrown child, and a drunk to boot."

"That's totally not fair. I admit when you guys met, he was in a dark period, but since then, he's really turned it around. His career has taken off, and his intentions toward her seem honest enough to me. My brother is clearly smitten with her and, considering the way she kept smiling at him, the attraction seemed mutual."

"You need to tell him to back off."

"They are two consenting adults. It's not any of my business. Besides, Lee should be dating. She's young still and probably wants to get married some day and maybe have more kids. Devin is not always my favorite person, but he's still a catch."

Jim stopped walking. "Unbelievable. I cannot believe you would condone this."

"Why are you so angry? And why do I have to be the one to say anything? Why don't you tell Lee how you feel?"

"Don't worry. I plan to." His face was stony as he turned away from me on the sidewalk. "Abigail, I'm not going to be able to make it to dinner after all." His long legs carried him toward the train without a glance back.

Later that evening, after canceling our dinner plans, I found myself wrapped in a blanket on the porch, pouring myself another glass of wine, calling my mother.

"Hi, sweetheart. Is anything wrong? Didn't you and Jim have dinner plans? Did little David enjoy the game today?"

"Jim had to work. The game was a lot of fun. But, Mom..." I started to cry.

"What's wrong?"

"I don't know if he had to work. We ran into Devin at the game. Did you know he lives next door to Lee now? They were super flirty together. Jim got really mad about it. He told me I had to tell Devin to leave her alone and then stormed off. How is any of this my fault?"

"I did know Devin was her neighbor and they've been spending some time together. Devin seems really taken with her. She's so attractive, it's no surprise. I'm sorry about Jim. He's always seemed very protective about her."

"You could say that again. Never half so protective about me, though." Bitterness took hold of me.

"I don't think that's true, dear. Besides, you are perfectly capable of taking care of yourself. You know, he's under a lot of stress. Just let him cool off and things will be fine."

"Okay, thanks, Mom. I have to go." Throwing the phone down, and burying my head in the pillows of the chair, huge sobs racked my body.

"Abby? Is everything okay?" Oblivious in my despair, I had not heard Jake come through the fence and up the porch.

"What are you doing here? Didn't you have a date?" I gulped, trying to gain control of my emotions.

"I did...do. I just forgot my phone and ran back to get it. Nicole is sitting with some friends at the bar down the street. You were crying so loudly. Sorry, I shouldn't have come over. You clearly want some privacy." He turned to go back down the stairs and then stopped. "Listen, if you need to talk, I can stay. I'll just shoot her a text and say something came up."

Avoiding eye contact, I tried to smooth my hair back into place and gracefully wipe away the snot pooling under my nose. "That would make you a terrible date."

"Probably...but it would make me an awesome

friend. This isn't about us hanging out together, is it? I shouldn't have said anything today. I didn't mean to start something between you guys."

"No, no. It's not. He didn't care about that at all." A hysterical sob filled giggle took hold of me.

Jake smiled ruefully, looking down at the near empty wine bottle on the small table. "Not to be a nag but how much wine have you had? And did you have any dinner? I find it's important to balance the two off each other, especially when you only weigh like a hundred pounds."

"That's not nice of you." My drunk's sense of injustice was high. "I've always been too skinny."

"No, no. That's not what I meant, Abby. You look amazing."

I stopped trying to pull my hair back and looked up at him. "You think so?"

His gaze grazed over me from head to toe. "Trust me, you look amazing...even with your eyes puffy and wearing a blanket. You're beautiful."

My sense of equilibrium dissolved under his steady gaze and I looked away. "You're right. I should eat something. And probably get to bed. Go enjoy your date and all the celebrations," I said, nodding into the surrounding darkness. The yells from the neighboring bars could be heard in the distance. "Thanks for stopping though, friend." My hand stretched out in a goodwill gesture. He took it and pulled me up.

Taking a moment before letting go, his thumb brushed across my palm. "Anytime, friend."

****

I woke up in the middle of the night as Jim crawled into bed beside me. "Abby, you awake?"

"Sort of." My voice croaked.

"I'm sorry about getting so upset earlier. I just think Lee needs to be careful after everything she's been through."

"I understand, but my brother is not the villain you're trying to make him out to be."

He ignored me. "I talked to Lee. She says there's nothing between them besides being neighbors. I believe her. It's your brother that is trying to turn it into something it's not. Luckily, she's not having any of it."

I grunted. This was at odds with what my mother had told me. Lee was likely keeping the truth from Jim to assuage his anger, a tactic with which I was well familiar.

"I'm glad things are okay. Let's get some sleep."

Chapter 9

The weather suddenly turned wet and cold. I rarely saw Jake any more. He was probably watching the playoff games inside, but it didn't seem right to invite myself over. Jim was away even more, often sleeping on the couch in his office. I joined a running club to occupy myself and hopefully make a few friends along the way.

After Thanksgiving, I started to look forward to all the holiday parties. Christmas was truly my favorite time of year. I made plans to go to Zoo Lights with Devin and Lee. In the past few months, they were spending more time together though I was uncertain how deep their connection ran. My own work holiday party would be small, just the associates, no spouses. Jim's law office, however, did a blowout gala every year. This year, the firm had rented out the Field Museum. There would be a band and dancing. I looked forward to wearing a new gown and getting all glammed up and seeing the exhibits after dark. It was a night I could be with Jim and meet the people he spent so much time with.

Jim finished getting ready before me and headed downstairs. He had arranged a black car to pick us up and I was rushing to get ready before it arrived. The black bias-cut dress clung across my spare frame. My hair had been curled in gentle waves, and my lips were stained a daring red color that made me feel sexy. Teetering in my heels, I navigated the stairs slowly, waiting for Jim to notice me. His first focus was my shoes.

"Are you sure you're going to be able to stand in those all night?"

"Yes, I'll be fine…Do you like the dress?" I looked at him hopefully and jutted my hip out.

"Sure, you look nice enough. Ready?" He draped my grandmother's old fur coat across my shoulders. It made me feel like a 1940s starlet. Jim curled his lip and said, "Don't you have a new coat to wear? That looks a little worn out."

"I love this coat. It used to be Nana's."

Shrugging, Jim opened the door and we stepped outside, making our way down the path to the car. A couple strolled down the sidewalk in front of the house, arms wrapped tightly around each other. Squinting in the dark, I realized it was Nicole and Jake. Since he had found me in tears all those months ago, Jake and I had only exchanged small talk in passing. I had seen Nicole coming and going, and was happy he'd met someone. She seemed nice enough. Jake stopped short in front of me and stared.

"Wow."

Nicole glanced at him, furrowing her brow at his enthusiasm. "You look so pretty, Abigail! Where are you guys going?"

Jim smiled at Nicole, nodding in my direction. "Holiday party and we're running late, thanks to this one. Have a good night you two."

Jake had not broken the stare between us. The waiting car was blocking traffic on the narrow street.

Jim tugged at my elbow, steadying me on the slippery stone. I folded myself awkwardly into the car, feeling Jake's eyes on me.

Jim ignored me the rest of the way, engaged with his phone. For once, I didn't initiate any conversation. Jake's reaction had rattled me, his attraction blatant. Why couldn't my husband see me that way?

The party was in full swing when we arrived. There were ice sculptures and soft lighting. There was a martini station and efficient waiters passing hors d'ouevres. It was all very festive and I felt myself getting excited. We circulated around the party for a bit, stopping to talk to different couples, a few of the faces familiar from previous years. We made the usual small talk and moved on. When I saw Eliza Stanton across the room, I looked at Jim in surprise.

"Why you didn't tell me Eliza works here? Or is it her husband?"

"Eliza. I've actually been working with her quite a bit lately. I didn't know you two knew each other." Jim seemed guarded suddenly.

"Oh, not well, but I've always liked her. Her father, you know he runs Castle, the hedge fund, he's a big donor of my father's and I've run into her quite a few times at fundraisers. Let's go over and say hi."

We walked over and I reached up and gave Eliza a hug. "It's so nice to see you again! How are the holidays? Are you doing anything special for Hanukkah?"

Eliza smiled at me and then looked up at Jim. "Just the usual over the top family gathering. What about you guys? I'm assuming you do a big Christmas dinner. You have such a big family, I'm sure it's a madhouse.

Do you know my husband, Brian?"

"We've met once or twice." I turned and smiled. Brian nodded at me with a disinterested expression and continued to nurse his scotch.

Eliza grabbed Jim's elbow. "Do you mind if I steal your husband for a bit? I have to talk to him about something work related for a minute."

They walked off to a corner without waiting for a response. I looked at Brian. "How long has Eliza been at the firm? Jim didn't tell me she was working here."

Brian looked surprised to see me still standing next to him. His eyes were glassy with alcohol, his body wavering as he replied, the tone bitter. "Since last winter. It feels like longer. I don't even see her anymore."

"I know, I feel like a widow a lot of the time too. They do like to keep long hours, but I guess that's how you get to the top. What do you do?"

His expression was sullen. "Doesn't it bother you? Not knowing what your husband is up to all those late nights?"

"Nope, I just assume he's working. If you'll excuse me, I have to run to the ladies." I walked away quickly, glancing at Jim and Eliza, not wanting to interrupt their deep conversation. I circled around, looking for other familiar faces, and thought about Eliza's husband. Eliza had always been very flirtatious. She was a beautiful and extremely rich woman who did as she pleased. It would be hard to partner with someone like that. Besides his dedication to work, Jim had never given me cause for jealousy. I could give him credit where credit was due. He was a loyal husband, even if he could be maddeningly inattentive.

A heavy arm around my shoulder pulled me from my thoughts. "Hello, pretty lady. Are you looking for a dance partner by any chance?" I looked up at Jim, his biggest smile focused solely on me. It felt wonderful.

"I certainly am, but only if he's tall, dark and handsome, with blue eyes."

"I happen to fit the bill." His hand in mine, we headed out to the dance floor. The rest of the night passed in a blur. There was drinking and dancing and lots of laughter between us. It was one of the nicest evenings we had ever spent together. On the car ride home, I snuggled into him, slightly over-served on champagne.

"I had a wonderful time. Thank you."

"You were great, Abby, the perfect wife. That political family of yours sure trained you well at small talk."

The reference to my family stung a bit. It would have been nicer if the compliment had stopped with me. "That's not true. I tried to make small talk with Brian, Eliza's husband. That didn't go well at all."

Jim looked down at me, my face still pressed into his shoulder. "What is that supposed to mean?"

"Well, he seemed very drunk and quite jealous. I don't know if it was of you or how many hours Eliza spends at work. I've only met Brian a handful of times. He's always in the wings at every event. I suppose it can get tiresome."

"Did he say he was specifically jealous of me? Why would he say that to my wife?"

"Well, no, he asked if I was ever jealous, and said something about never seeing his wife since she started working at the firm. Honestly, he was slurring his words. It didn't make a lot of sense to me."

Jim didn't reply to that and I dozed off in the comfortable backseat. We went upstairs, still holding hands, and made love for the first time in a long time, with a tenderness that felt different. Entwined with each other and the sheets, we fell asleep together.

I awoke in the morning with a groggy head, my eyes crusted with last night's makeup. Jim looked at me, all smiles. A sense of contentment filled me.

"It's Sunday, and we don't have to be anywhere until dinner at Lee's. What should we do today?"

"For how long do I have you?" I asked doubtfully. "How many hours of work do you want to squeeze in?"

"None. The whole damn firm is hungover and expecting nothing from me. Why don't we go to breakfast, then finish up some Christmas shopping. Christmas is in two days and I haven't even thought about it."

"Well, I have and most of the presents for our family are wrapped and under the tree, including my present to you."

"Then we can just shop for your present today. I'd like to get you something nice this year."

"That's really sweet. You don't have to."

"I want to. Get dressed. We can take the train down to Michigan Avenue."

Pulling on a pair of jeans and washing my face, I hurried downstairs, not wanting to break the spell. This new attentive version of my husband was a delightful surprise. Maybe if we just carved out enough time for each other, the closeness we'd once had would come back. "I'm ready." I reached for my striped puffer jacket. Jim hated the coat but it was a cold day and it would keep me warm walking around downtown.

"Oh, no, not that thing."

"I love this coat. It has a million pockets so I don't even need to bring a purse."

"Okay, okay. I'm only agreeing because I'm too hungover to fight with you today."

I grinned. "That's so kind of you. You ready?"

Out the door, we walked to the train, still holding hands and making small talk about the party. As we turned onto the main drag, there was a couple before us, kissing quickly over a small boy's head. It was Lee, David below her, staring at a toy in the window display.

"Hey, guys! Devin!" My brother swiveled his head toward us. I looked over at Jim, his features tense. I had mentioned Devin and Lee had been spending time together, but not that they were full on dating.

"Hey, sis, Jim, what brings you guys out on such a cold day?"

"We were just heading downtown to do a little last minute Christmas shopping. David, are you excited for Christmas?" Bending down, my mind was whirring, trying to think of a way to diffuse the situation. Jim's glare was boring holes into Lee, his disapproval evident.

"Lee, when you told me you were seeing someone, I didn't expect this." Jim's voice was like a razor.

"Well, surprise. What can I say? Devin living across the hall just makes it so convenient." Lee looked around awkwardly, catching my eyes in a pleading smile.

"That's great. You guys have known each other for years, right? It's natural that you would get together. Lee, maybe you could come to Christmas dinner at my parents' house? They would love to see you and my cousin's kids would adore playing with David." An overly enthusiastic grin remained plastered to my face as I avoided making eye contact with either of the men.

Devin looked at me. "I've been trying to convince Lee of the same thing, actually. She had planned on spending Christmas in her apartment, which just seems depressing. What do you say, Lee? Please?"

Lee smiled tightly, still avoiding Jim's eyes. "Sure, why not? Something different this year. Would you like to go to a big party for Christmas, darling?" She bent to pick up David, his little body puffed up in a snowsuit.

The little boy clapped his chubby toddler hands. "Presents? Auntie, you zoo animal."

"Ha!" my brother exclaimed, embracing the lighthearted comment. "You sure do look like a zoo animal. Where on earth did you get that hideous thing?"

"I bought it at that store with all the hiking gear on Southport. I will have you know this brand of jacket is one of Oprah's favorite things and animal print is very hot this year. But it's a Christmas miracle, you and Jim are finally in agreement on something. He also hates it."

Lee smiled. "Well, in my opinion, it's cute. Maybe I'll go see if they have any left in my size."

"We'd better catch the train. Lee, Devin." Jim leaned over and gave David a little high five. "Sounds like I'll be seeing you at Christmas, little man."

Conversation remained at a standstill as we walked the block to the station. The train was rumbling in the distance. The announcement board said it was due in two minutes. We sprinted, running up the stairs and cramming onto the crowded train. The press of people around us made any discussion impossible. Holding on to the pole, I focused on staying upright.

As we exited the train a few stops later, I steeled myself, deciding to bend the truth in an effort to clear the air. "I had no idea they were dating. Neither my mother nor Devin mentioned it. I was not keeping this from you."

"I know you weren't. It was just a surprise that Lee kept it a secret. She wouldn't say who she was dating. Proximity breeds familiarity. Look, I'm not that upset. Maybe you're right. He's not nearly as obnoxious as he used to be. The important thing is that he treats them well."

Relief rolled through me. I would not have to spend the holidays keeping them in their separate corners. "I'm really happy you feel that way. If nothing else, it will be fun to see David for Christmas. Maybe we could find a Santa suit for you somewhere—"

"Not a chance, Abigail. Mind if we stop and get some coffee?"

The rest of the day passed pleasantly. Jim bought me some pearl earrings I had been eyeing for a while. As we were discussing whether to get dinner downtown, Jim got a text from Eliza asking him to come into the office and finish up something they had been working on.

"Do you mind, Abby?"

"Not at all." I smiled. "Thank you for my earrings and this day. It was a treat getting to spend so much time with you."

Jim looked at me thoughtfully. "I'm glad. I'm trying to make this a pleasant Christmas for you." He hailed a passing cab. "See you at home."

I decided to do some more shopping and call my mother.

"Hey, Mom. How are you? Did you think of anything else you want me to pick up for Christmas dinner?"

After making a mental note of her requests, I mentioned we had run into Devin and Lee. "Did you know they were dating, Mother?"

"I did. He told me not to say anything. Lee was worried about Jim's reaction. Does he know? Was he there too?"

"Yes, he does know, and honestly, he was surprisingly okay with it. It sounds like Lee and David are going to join us for Christmas."

"That's wonderful news. Devin has been quite smitten with her for a while. Even before they started dating, he was at their apartment a lot, spending time with her and the boy. I never would have expected it, but maybe becoming a stepfather will be the making of him. He seems quite ready to step into the role."

"Mom, you're totally jumping the gun."

"Well, maybe, but a mother can hope. Lee is such a mystery. She's so reserved, but if she's letting him spend so much time with her son, I have to think it must be serious."

"I'm happy for both of them if it works out. Okay, Mom, I have to go. See you Tuesday."

Two days later, it was Christmas, and we were driving up to Winnetka. Devin and Lee were coming up separately, after David's nap. I looked at Jim, sitting behind the wheel.

"I'm glad Lee has decided to join us and it's great that you're taking their relationship in stride." My hands clenched in my lap. "Maybe there's a chance you and Devin could bury the hatchet?"

"That's going a bit far, don't you think?" He looked sideways at me. "There's no way we're going to become best buds or anything. I just think it's time Lee found someone. If nothing else, he can afford her."

"What's that supposed to mean?"

"Just that you are a family of means, and he, at least, is no longer a deadbeat. He can support David and Lee financially. Don't read anything into it, Abby."

"Lee seems to be doing fine as a paralegal, though. She doesn't seem to live beyond her means." Jim had been forthright about helping Lee out when there had been extra bills and money was tight, but now I wondered about the extent of it. Our finances had always been kept separate. If he was helping her, it was really his business, but it made me feel like I had been left in the dark.

"Right. She's doing fine. Kids are just expensive, that's all."

"Well, it's wonderful you're being positive about the whole thing, whatever the reason. My mom says he's really taken with her."

We sank back into silence during the rest of the drive up Sheridan Road, the startling blue of Lake Michigan breaking out between the houses. It was a beautiful, clear day. The sun warmed my face through the glass. There had been no snow yet, though it had been forecast for later in the week. I felt a childish disappointment that it wouldn't be a white Christmas.

My parents' house was overflowing with people and holiday decorations when we arrived. My mother rushed over to greet us. "Come in, come in! Are Devin and Lee with you?"

"No, they decided to let David take a little nap first, before all the excitement."

"Good thinking. I'm just so excited Lee decided to join us. Devin was so hurt when she didn't come up for Thanksgiving."

"He didn't mention it to me. I didn't realize he had invited her up. He really had to twist her arm to get her to come up this time. Jim was the one who encouraged it, actually." My husband stood a few steps ahead of me, easily chatting with my father.

"Abigail," my dad called. "We were just talking about going out to visit Tommy in California, maybe in March, enjoy some sunshine while it's rainy and cold here. What do you two think? We could rent a big house by the beach. I brought it up to Will and Devin the other day. They love the idea."

"That actually sounds like a lot of fun, Dad. What do you think, Jim?"

"You should definitely go, Abby."

"Well, I want both of you to go," my father stated.

"I understand, sir, but I doubt I'll be able to get away. It would be a nice distraction for Abby."

"A distraction? What's that supposed to mean?"

Jim looked at me. "I know my crazy work schedule makes you feel a little lonely at times and in spring, that is likely to be worse."

I wondered at the gravity in his tone. "Well, we can talk about it later. You could probably get away for at least a few days."

The men went into the living room and I followed my mother into the kitchen. "How are things, Abby? You and Jim seemed very happy when you walked in.

Is he really working that much?"

"He is, but with the holidays, things have been slower. It's actually been lovely. We've spent more time together in the past week than we usually do in a month. He's like a different person. I can't explain it."

"Well, I'm glad for you, dear. You look like you're glowing. You're not expecting, are you?"

"Ha, no, not to my knowledge. Though that would be a wonderful surprise. We haven't really talked about having kids recently. Like I said, usually he's so busy."

"Well, at least we get to spend some time with David today. If Devin marries Lee, I get a bonus grandson, which would be wonderful. Are you and she getting along better?"

"Some…we're cordial with each other, but there's no real friendship there. I know this sounds snarky, and I really am happy for Devin if he's happy, but it seems like she's worming her way into all these different parts of my life. She and Jim have always spent so much time together, now Devin is falling all over himself for her. I know I'm being unkind but I just wish I trusted her more."

"Well, that does sound a bit dramatic. Perhaps now that she's not alone, she might feel more secure with you. Unhappiness can make people standoffish. Being a single mother is no easy feat."

"You're right, Mom. As always." My mother bent down to check the roast in the oven. Would I ever be like my mother, a brooding hen reveling in feeding all her little chickens?

Jim stuck his head in the kitchen. "Devin and Lee have arrived. Your dad suggested we give David one of his Christmas presents so he has something to keep him entertained. Do you want to come with me and give it to him?"

"Yes, sounds fun. I'll be right there. Mom, you coming?"

We followed Jim into the living room. Devin had a possessive hand on Lee's shoulder. David was sitting on the floor, struggling with the wrapping paper. "Here, let me help you, little man." Jim sat down with him.

"I'm glad you guys are here." We all exchanged hugs. "This is actually your first time here, right?"

"Yes, it is. Thank you for including us. It just seemed too lonely to stay home alone with David, especially now that he's old enough to enjoy the holidays."

Jim and David were still kneeling on the floor. The gift was some sort of fire truck and Jim was showing him how to work the lights and which buttons to press for the sound. Jim looked up at Lee. "I'm glad you decided to come this year too. If you have a second, I'd like to speak to you about something in private."

Concern flickered across Lee's face. "Of course, I hope it's nothing serious."

Devin looked between Jim and Lee suspiciously. "What can you possibly have to say to her today, on Christmas, that can't be said in front of everyone else?"

Jim tensed. "Clearly, something that has nothing to do with you. Please, Lee, I'd like to talk to you. Will you come to the library with me?"

Lee looked over at me. "Sure, Jim. Do you mind keeping an eye on David, Abby?"

"Of course." They walked down the long hallway to the library together.

Devin looked at me. "I know he's your husband,

Abby, but I'd really like to deck that guy one. The demands he puts on you and on her are so ridiculous. He has to have absolute and total control over everyone. Do you know why she didn't come to Thanksgiving? I asked her. She didn't want Jim to think our relationship was that serious. Honestly, I don't even think she had told him about us. What right does that clown have telling her who to date? God, he's so full of himself."

"I'm sorry, Devin. When we were driving up today, Jim said he actually approved of the two of you guys dating. Maybe he just wants to tell Lee that in private?" My tone was hopeful but Devin just shook his head.

When Jim and Lee returned fifteen minutes later, she looked pale and drawn. Devin approached her, the concern on his face apparent. "What was that about?" I questioned my husband.

"Nothing, just something that needed to be said. Don't worry about it, Abby. It's none of your concern."

"Was this about Devin? You just said he was good for her and for David."

"It's none of your goddamn business," he snapped, stepping away and going to sit by my father and other brothers across the room.

Soon after, we all sat down to Christmas dinner. No one else had noticed the battle lines being drawn. David was between Devin and Lee. Jim and I sat at the far end of the table. Jim pointedly reserved his conversation for my grandfather on his left. His tone had left me angry and I struggled to engage with my brother Will's wife, Carol, on my right. Stealing glances at Lee, I thought she seemed ill at ease, fussing unnecessarily over her little boy. Devin's jaw was set in a hard line.

Before dessert was served, Lee stood up and announced it was getting late and she wanted to keep David on his bedtime schedule. They packed up to leave. Jim and I stayed on through dessert, engaged in a lively conversation about the new immigration bill the House was proposing. After helping my mom carry plates to the sink, Jim came and found me. "I'd like to head out, if that's okay with you."

The first part of the drive was silent, the argument weighing on me, until I could hold it in no longer. "Is Lee okay? What was it all about?"

"Oh, nothing, Abigail. Just some family news. It's rather personal. She wouldn't want me sharing it with anyone. Seriously, everything is fine." He smiled at me. "Your mother really outdid herself with the roast this year. I should've loosened my belt before we got in the car."

Chapter 10

The days following Christmas had been strange between Jim and me. Since his talk with Lee, it felt like he was pulling away from me. Likely he felt betrayed since I had dared to question him. The magic we'd had before the holiday was gone and the chasm between us grew. My office was working from home over the holiday, since most people had kids at home for school break. Sitting in the kitchen, I was busy answering emails on my computer at the kitchen table when Jim came downstairs. He cleared his throat behind me, waiting to be acknowledged. My ire rose. He would have been affronted if I had been the one to interrupt his work. I continued typing on the keyboard.

"Hey, Abigail. Can you take a break? We need to talk." Angrily, my body rotated in the chair to face him. "It's over between us. I want a divorce and I want it to be as amicable as possible. We don't have kids. It should be relatively straightforward."

"What the hell are you talking about?" My breath froze in my chest. "What have I done to cause you to want a divorce?"

"I just don't love you like that, Abigail. I never did."

"You're just realizing this now? We've been together for six years. I paid your way through law school and put up with all your bullshit, all the nights studying. And since then, since you started your big old career, I've never asked you to do a damn thing. I'm the one who gets groceries, picks up the dry cleaning, always the perfect uncomplaining wife, putting my own career on the back burner. That means nothing to you? Because I did it out of love, and now you tell me there is nothing between us."

"That's just it, Abigail," he said, the repeated use of my full name hitting me like a slap with every syllable. "You're perfect. Perfectly bred, perfectly mannered and pedigreed. You're like a goddamn show pony. You're not a real person, just a caricature of some 1940s politician's wife, and I can't stand it any longer. I want passion with someone who is alive. Someone who is not just ambitious for me, but for herself. For God's sake, even sex with you is goddamn systematic. It's like you have no real desire in you. You're just a brittle, boring wasp of a woman I married because it improved my trajectory in life."

I stood up, clutching the edge of the table. His vile synopsis of my character had left me shaking. How could I have been so blind?

"I'm sorry, Abs." His tone softened. "That was too harsh. It wasn't all bad. When we first met, there was a genuine connection. It just wasn't enough to justify a lifetime together." He paused and put his hand on my shoulder. "I've met someone. She is beautiful, aggressive, and driven. She makes me feel alive. It's been transformative."

"Who is she?" I looked up sharply.

"It doesn't matter, it just matters that it's happening."

"You might as well tell me her name. Is it someone

from work?"

"Abigail…."

The Christmas party flashed into my mind. "Eliza Stanton. It's Eliza, isn't it? Oh my God, I saw you two in the corner talking at the holiday party. You were arguing."

Jim looked at me, taking a deep breath. "Yes, she was telling me I needed to end it with you or she would tell you about the affair. What she and I have comes along once in a lifetime. I need to pursue this, whatever happens. We don't have children together, Abby. We can both start again, make a clean break of things."

The reference to my infertility stung me. My voice grew steely. "So, the only woman who could have replaced me is Eliza Stanton, daughter of the richest man in Chicago. Is her daddy throwing in a plush job as head counsel at his hedge fund for the dowry? Come on, let's get real. Life is just one giant ladder for you to climb and this one is bigger than the one you're on now. I've just outlived my usefulness." A visceral pain gripped my body, knowing I had been willfully deceiving myself this whole time.

"I'm sorry, Abigail." He picked up his gym bag and briefcase and headed to the door. "I've got to get to work. For what it's worth, I had intended to let you down more gently. This will be good for both of us, you'll see."

Outside the front window, the snow was being hurled through space with gale force winds. The winter storm forecasted earlier in the week had finally arrived. There was at least a foot of snow on the ground and the roads were impassable. Jim would be taking the El, the only form of transportation with a chance of getting through the storm.

"I hate you. How's that for passion? I hope the train careens off the track and bursts into flames." Anger and shame made me lash out.

"Nice, Abigail. You might crack in two showing so much emotion. You best be careful."

Glaring at me, he reached for his bag, ready with his suit neatly folded inside for him to change into at work. His appearance would be immaculate, despite the storm. "I will be back later to pack a few things and start labeling stuff so the movers can come by and box it. Goodbye, Abs."

With that, he walked out of our marriage. Rage took hold of me. He had accused me of being a shell of a woman, the proverbial doormat. I wouldn't let him get off so easily now. Throwing on my boots and my black-and-white striped anorak, I took off running after him.

"Fuck you!" I shouted, chasing him down the street. Without stopping, using all my momentum, I shoved him hard in the back. "You have until midnight tonight to get your stuff out or I'm giving it away, all your fancy Italian suits and shoes, your college sports treasures, every last bit of it."

"Fine, Abby, as you wish."

His calm further goaded me. The storm was swirling around us, the wind so intense it was a struggle to breathe. I let out a primordial scream and went careening wildly into him, but this time, he was prepared. He shoved his elbow into my chest and I lost my balance, slipping on the icy sidewalk, landing hard.

He just shook his head, turned, and walked away. I sat there stunned, feeling the bruise forming on my hip, trying to slow the beating in my chest.

Watching him cross the street and cut through the alley to the shortcut to the train station, I decided to follow him. At the mouth of the alley, his tall form was already disappearing in the distance. The snow was piling up in drifts and I no longer had the strength for the chase when I saw my car. Both entrances to the alley had been blocked last night, one side by a construction crew, the other a moving van and I had parked on the street. Sinking into the driver's seat, I turned the car over. A vague desire to drive home, to Winnetka, and curl up in my mother's lap like a small child drifted through my consciousness. Slipping and sliding, the car struggled to inch its way out of the tight spot, my visibility nonexistent as the windshield wipers hopelessly tried to clear a wall of snow on the glass. Going on would be a suicide mission. The roads were likely impassable. Putting the car back in park, sobs wracked my body. I was stuck, literally and metaphorically, left behind by my husband to fend for myself as he beat a hasty departure from our life together.

The tears fell relentlessly, and I lost my sense of time. Sirens cut through the quiet, stopping nearby, snapping me back to consciousness. I took a deep breath, wiped my face, and braced myself for the snowy walk back up the block to the house.

At home, I mechanically removed my coat and shoes and went upstairs. One of his expensive work shirts was hanging out of the hamper. Grabbing it, my hands gripped the fabric trying to rip it apart without success. I gave up and instead hugged it to my chest, smelling his deodorant, woodsy and clean. I wrapped it around me like a security blanket and fell into bed, succumbing to a deep and bottomless sleep.

The doorbell cut through my dreamless state, bringing me back to reality with a thud. Confused about the time, I wondered if I had missed my afternoon meeting. Was someone from the office checking on me?

Pulling myself out of bed, I dragged myself downstairs and answered the door. The snow was still falling and the front stoop was knee deep. A police officer had waded through it and was now standing before me.

"Mrs. Hardy?"

"Yes, can I help you?" My fingers combed through my hair, trying to smooth it down.

"My name is Officer Jenkins." He flashed his badge at me. "Ma'am, we're sorry to inform you that your husband has passed away."

"Wait, what? How? I just saw him this morning. He was on his way to the train."

"He fell in the path of the oncoming train. We are pulling station footage to see if he just slipped with the icy conditions or if there were other circumstances."

"What other circumstances? Oh God, this is horrible. Jim…." My voice trailed off, my knees weak. "I have to sit down."

"Of course. We are just doing a routine investigation to see if there was foul play. May I come in and take a statement from you?"

"Yes, yes, of course." I opened the door wider and he trailed in after me.

Limp, I sat down on the couch next to the officer and stared at the opposite wall. There was a photo of us on our honeymoon. We had gone on safari. In the picture, we are resting in a hammock together, my head on his chest, with the glorious colors of an African sunset behind us. The trip had been a wedding present from my parents, who had insisted we take an elaborate vacation before settling down to married life. It would be years before we could take any significant vacation with his career and potential children on the horizon. The trip had been amazing. We had been so enthralled with the landscape and the intimacy of being out in the Savannah, glamping in those fabulous cabins, romantically sleeping under the stars. We had been so happy together then. Or maybe I had just thought we were happy. It felt like all my memories were false. He'd left me only this morning, never to return again. I would never see him again. "This can't be real, this can't be happening…."

"Can I get you something, Mrs. Hardy? A glass of water?"

"No, no thank you."

"Mrs. Hardy, you seem to be experiencing some shock. Is there someone you can call?"

I stared up at him blankly and then closed my eyes. "My dad. I'd like to call my dad." I reached into my pocket for the cell phone I'd remembered to retrieve from the car and called my dad's office.

"Is the senator in? This is his daughter." I saw the police officer draw in a breath at my words.

"Oh, of course, I'll try him at home."

"Goddamn snow." I tried their landline at home. "Mom? Oh, Mom." Hearing her voice immediately reduced me to a small child, desperate for comfort. "Is Dad there? Jim's been killed on the El and, oh, I don't

144

know what to do. The police are here. No, I don't have any details." The tears started coming down harder and I leaned my head forward, gasping. The phone fell out of my hand.

My mother's voice tumbled down away from me, yelling, "Abby, calm down. We're on our way."

The officer stood up. "Perhaps you could text them and have them meet us at the station. We're going to need you to come in and identify the body."

I nodded, willing myself to stand. My legs carried me to the front door, my striped print jacket still heaped on the floor next to it. The coat seemed so ridiculous now as I pulled it on quickly. It had seemed like a fun addition to my wardrobe when I'd bought it, and then soon found that every other woman in Lakeview had the same thought this winter. Now it was as if we were a herd of zebras crisscrossing the urban tundra in unison. I considered asking the officer to allow me a few minutes to go upstairs to find a staid black coat, the widow's mantle, rather than parading into the morgue in this monstrosity, but it didn't really matter what I wore. It wouldn't make a bit of difference.

A loud banging at the front door made me jump. I looked back at the officer, panicked. The officer stepped forward. "Would you like me to get it? Are you expecting someone? Your parents?"

"No, they wouldn't be here yet. They're coming from the suburbs. I can get it." I opened the door. "Devin!"

"Mom called and told me what happened. Are you okay?" He grabbed me in a big bear hug, breathing heavily, likely having sprinted the two blocks from his apartment to my house. I was grateful for the short distance. His familiar presence gave me strength. "How did he die?"

"He slipped off the platform they think. It was so icy. He was so insistent to get to the office no matter what the weather. He thought it made him look good. I just don't know. The police are looking into it. I have to go and identify him. Will you come?"

"Of course, absolutely. Is that okay?" He looked back at the officer behind me. The officer nodded.

"I can take you guys over. The car is parked outside."

As the police car carried us up the slick streets to the station a few blocks away, I wondered if they had called his office and if his new paramour was aware of his death. Lee and David, they would both be devastated. I made a mental note to go over there and break the news in person. That poor little boy. What would they do without Jim's presence in their life?

We arrived at the station. Devin walked ahead of me to speak with the officers and then came back. "The body is probably not going to be in great shape. Why don't you let me identify him? They are going to put you in a room and ask you some questions."

I stared at him, the tears starting again. He was probably right, seeing Jim would be heart wrenching, his large form broken and crushed. "Okay, thanks, Devin. I really mean it."

They put me in a room, bringing me a cup of black coffee, hot and watered down.

I cringed drinking it and then chided myself for caring about the taste of the coffee when Jim was dead. Lost in my thoughts, time seemed to stand still. The door thumped open and I jumped, surprised to find myself still in this drab little room.

"Hello, I'm Detective Radanovic," said an immensely tall man, filling the doorway. He moved cautiously into the room, as if his sheer bulk would send objects flying. He sat down heavily across from me and my stomach clenched.

"I'm sorry about your husband, Mrs. Hardy."

"Thank you. It's been quite a shock. Why have I been here so long? Was my brother not able to identify Jim?" His name felt odd in my mouth, my general sense of unease growing as the detective seemed to avoid all eye contact.

"Mrs. Hardy, were you on good terms with your husband?"

"How is that your business?"

"Mrs. Hardy, that's a very unique coat you have on."

"Excuse me, how is this relevant? What does my coat have to do with anything?"

"Mrs. Hardy, I'm going to show you a video we pulled from the station's CCTV footage. The video clearly shows your husband being pushed by a woman in a zebra patterned parka."

I leaned forward in my chair and watched in horror as the scene played out on the cramped screen of his computer. "He was pushed?"

"Mrs. Hardy, was there a reason you would be angry enough to push your husband to his death?"

"Wait, what, no, that's not me. You think I did that? That coat is the hot accessory of the year. Everyone is wearing it this season. Why do you think that's me? You can't even see the person's face."

"Did the two of you have a fight this morning? Is

there a reason you would be angry enough to kill him?"

Suddenly the air in the room seemed to evaporate. Struggling, I ground out the truth, knowing it was better to be honest than labeled a liar later. "We were getting a divorce. Jim announced it this morning, before leaving for the train, that he was having an affair and wanted to marry his mistress. I was upset, but not enough to murder him. What would I have to gain by killing him? He was out of my life either way."

"Did you follow your husband to the train station?"

"Briefly yes, but I ended up stopping at my car. It was parked on the street. The alley was blocked last night and I couldn't get to my garage. I had considered driving back to my parents' house, but then with the snow, it was impossible to drive anywhere this morning. I just grabbed my phone and went back to my house."

"So you did not have your phone on your person all morning? The GPS then would not be able to support your claim that you did not go to the train station. Did you immediately return to the house with the phone?"

"No...no, I didn't. I was in shock. I sat there for a while, at least twenty minutes."

"Is it possible you had known ahead of time that your husband intended to leave you? So you left the car with the phone in it on the street as a sort of alibi?"

"No! No, no, no!!!" My body trembled at the accusation. "I just sat in the car and cried. How would I have known he was leaving me? It was a shock. I was just dazed and lost track of time." The severity of the situation hit me. "I will not speak to you any more without a lawyer present."

"Mrs. Hardy, you're free to go for now. Please don't leave town. I assure you, if it wasn't for your father's office, we would be charging you right now. As it stands, the DA is going to want an airtight case before he proceeds."

My knees slammed against the table as I shot up, gathering up my things, including my infernal jacket. I wanted to trash it, but realized doing that would look like an admission of guilt, an attempt to destroy evidence. A wave a nausea came over me. The detective opened the door. My father stood outside waiting.

"Daddy!" I cried, weak with relief, knowing my father would be able to help me.

"Let's not talk here, Abby. My car is waiting."

We headed toward the front door. "No, this way." My father grabbed my elbow and steered me down a narrow hallway, ushering me out of a back entrance into a parking garage. "The street is teeming with reporters." We slid into the back seat of the waiting SUV. "It's late. I'm taking you to Winnetka. There are reporters surrounding your place. Now tell me what happened."

"I don't know, I just don't know. This morning, Jim just started packing up his gym bag to take the train in because of the snowstorm, and then all of a sudden, he was telling me our marriage was over, he'd found someone else and wanted a divorce." My cheeks flushed with the shame of rejection.

"Wait, this morning? Before he died?" My father looked alarmed.

"Yes, we got into a fight. He tried to shut it down by leaving so I followed him. How pathetic am I? They think I followed him to the train station. There's footage from the train station of a woman in a coat like mine pushing him off the platform, but it wasn't me, Daddy!" My breath was shallow and the terror of the situation overwhelmed me.

My father's face, attempting to regain its standard poker expression, cracked for a brief instance, his fear for me clearly visible. "I believe you. We'll get the best defense lawyer in the city and private detectives to dig up whoever might have wanted to frame you. We will figure this out, Abigail." He pulled me close and we rode the rest of the way in silence.

Barriers had been set up by the local police on our street. There were a few stray reporters who had taken the initiative to come up to the North Shore. They would leave after they had a picture of me, sneaking back into my parent's house after the brutal murder, eager to be the first with the image.

"Oh my baby," my mother cried out, opening the front door. The cameras were clicking furiously. Their questions blended into one loud roar behind me. My father ushered us in.

"Honey, what happened?" My mother folded her arms around me. "Are you okay?"

"No, nothing is okay. It's all a mess. I just don't understand any of it."

"Abigail needs to go rest. I'll fill you in while she goes upstairs and then I need to make some calls. Perhaps you could give her one of your sleeping pills, dear. It would be for the best." My mother nodded and followed me up the stairs.

"Here you go. Your father's right. You are in shock. Do you want me to call a doctor?"

"No, the pill is fine, Mom. I just want to lie down." My mother was flittering around me. It felt like a cocoon being woven. I felt safe but knew the feeling wouldn't last.

Upstairs in my room, I found some old sweats and lay down, swallowing the pill without water, willing it to work quickly.

Chapter 11

The morning light filtered in. It was early still. The wooliness of a medically induced sleep had addled my brain. Everything seemed surreal waking up in my childhood bedroom. Yesterday's nightmare came back to me. Throwing on a bathrobe, I headed downstairs. My father sat in the kitchen with his coffee, writing in a notebook.

"I've reached out to the lawyers. They will be here at ten to talk over strategy. It's only a matter of time until you are charged."

"Well, at least it's not an election year," I cracked feebly.

"Abby, this is serious. They are going to try to make an example of you. They can't be seen as soft in such a high-profile case. We need to focus on your defense."

"I know it is, Dad. I'm just in shock. Let me get some coffee then I'll sit and write down anything that might be useful. The conversation Jim and I had before…." I rubbed my forehead. There had to be some clue, somewhere. "Who would frame me? Maybe this isn't even about me. Did someone want to kill Jim and I was just a convenient scapegoat? It couldn't be his mistress. She had no reason to want him dead. Is it possible this is about trying to discredit you, to take down our whole family?"

"It's possible, but let's get back to the mistress. Who was he seeing? Someone you know?"

"You know her. Eliza Stanton, daughter of Peter Stanton. They worked together."

"This just keeps getting worse and worse."

"She can't possibly think I would have killed him." It hit me that most of Chicago was waking up to the morning paper, deciding that indeed, I would be a credible villain in this story. "I'm going up now. I'll be down at ten."

Dutifully, I went back to my room, taking pen and paper, and tried to write down verbatim what had transpired between Jim and me. There wasn't anything there that would clear me, only indict me. Thinking back over the past year or two, it occurred to me that Jim had always worked many late nights but it had definitely accelerated in the past 6 months. That must have been when his affair with Eliza had begun. Had there been others? Our sex life had a lot of dry spells. Perhaps other mistresses filled the void. We had spent so little time together in recent years.

How much did I really know about my husband's investment in this marriage? I had relished the sense of teamwork so established by my own parents and grandparents. The men were busy building careers and the women were the foundation, staying home, raising children. It all seemed so archaic now. Why had I thought that life would suit me? I had confused that arrangement with happiness, not recognized the fact that love was the reason for the happiness, the overwhelming love my father had for his wife, like his father before him. Blindly, I had overlooked the fact that Jim hadn't really loved me. For a while, Jim had been content with the arrangement as well, no doubt appreciating the benefit to his own career, but when he had met Eliza, he'd found his chance for real happiness. I should have left years ago, before he even proposed. At least then I wouldn't be in this predicament, accused of murdering a man who no longer cared for me, if he had ever cared at all.

My pen had stopped scratching the paper. I'd had no further insight into Jim's potential killer and the lawyers would be here any minute. I went down to meet them.

The meeting went on for an hour. The two men were impeccably dressed and remarkably similar. My mind was drifting and my father held up most of the conversation, sharing all the details of the previous day.

The men stood up to signal their departure. I stood in tandem, willing them to relay something positive regarding my innocence. They looked serious. "We will work tirelessly to clear you, but it does not look good. You've been placed at the scene and you had motive." The pain shot through my lip as I bit down, trying not to cry.

"Thank you for coming. I'll walk you out," said my father.

I sank back into the wingback chair in my father's study, before the lit fire, a wave of nostalgia taking hold. I had sat in that chair as a child, reading books while my father worked at his desk. A car honked outside. I stood up and looked out the window. The police were blockading the end of our street. News vans were lined up, waiting for a shot at seeing me. The lawyers' car crept slowly through the crowd.

It felt awful imposing on my family like this. The

circus following me had invaded not only my peace but my family's and their neighbors'. How long would it be before the news cameras would give up, bleeding dry the details of my life? My family was in it with me, but at least I could spare them living through the chaos outside their front door. I resolved to go home, pack a bag, move into a hotel, and do my best to remain anonymous in the process.

Leaving the library, I headed upstairs to find my mother. "Mom, you've been amazing. I love your support, but it's best if I go. It's not fair to you. As long as the reporters think I'm here, they are not going anywhere."

"That's ridiculous, Abby. Where will you go? They will just park outside your house instead. At least the police here have the flexibility to block off the street. They won't do that for you in the city."

"I can get a room at a hotel or go stay with Devin. God, has anyone talked to Lee? She must have been devastated."

"Yes, Devin broke the news to her after we picked you up from the station. He says she's very upset. She's been withdrawn, and somewhat hysterical. It's only natural. They seem to only have each other. I found Jim's father's number and left him a message. He did call me back. I'm to reach out again once we have the details of the funeral arranged. He will come if he's able. I didn't know whether to offer to buy him a plane ticket or if it would be rude."

I looked over at my mother. She could be the most thoughtful woman in the world. Calling Jim's father hadn't even occurred to me. "Oh, Mom, what would I do without you? I haven't even thought about the funeral or what he would want. I don't know where he put his will, though his lawyer would have a copy. Maybe it includes instructions for his burial or cremation or whatever…"

"Your father can reach out to his attorney. Just write down the name for me. I will organize everything for you." She paused. "I hate to say this, but even if he did want to be cremated, you should probably have some sort of wake or memorial for him. It would be good publicity to show you as the grieving widow." Her brow furrowed. She hated the duplicitous nature of appearances for appearance's sake, but considered them necessary.

"You're probably right and honestly, I would like to say goodbye to him too. Maybe it will give me a chance for closure. I've just been thrown into a fight for my life without getting to process his death."

Getting ready to leave, I reached for the now infamous jacket but thought better of it. I flipped through the coat closet in the hall, looking for a more somber option. My father joined us. "Where are you going? There's going to be just as much media in Lakeview as there is here."

"I know, but I need to go home and start going through Jim's things and pick out something for him to be laid out in. I don't have my work laptop, assuming I still have a job. There's just a lot to do. Thank you for bringing me here, but I just need to be back in my own space. Also, I'm hoping there might be some sort of clue in Jim's office back at the house…or tucked away in one of his drawers."

"It's a good idea. But just so you know, the police have already been through your house looking for evidence."

"Oh my God, I didn't even think of that. Of course. The house has probably been trashed." My throat was tight. "This is such a nightmare."

"You're not on your own, Abby. We're all going to work together to figure this out. Here, why don't you take your mother's black wool coat? I know it doesn't quite go with yoga pants, but it will look innocuous. I'll call my driver to take you home. He's been sitting down the street on standby. At least the back windows are blacked out."

After a few minutes, the car pulled into the driveway. As I exited the front door and ducked into the car, the reporters' screams escalated into a fevered pitch at the unexpected sighting. We drove through the hordes, and I was grateful for my father's driver. Fists banged on my window, demanding a quote, the sudden raps making me feel like an animal hounded and trapped.

As we turned onto Sheridan, I looked behind me to confirm the news vans were following us and began to strategize my exit from the car once we got to Lakeview. My father's driver, Louie, told me he would parallel park in front of my house and walk me to the gate. From there, I could dart down the gangway and through the kitchen door, out of sight of the reporters standing out front.

Thirty minutes later, we had reached my house; dozens of people were milling about on the sidewalk. Opening the car door, the noise overwhelmed me. I hunched into Louie's back as he elbowed his way through the crowd. I slipped through the gate alone, the ornamental relic from a hundred years ago doing nothing to shield me from the cameras. No one had come to shovel and the snow piled up, thick and slippery, impeding my progress. Inelegantly, I caught myself against the wall of the house, reporters recording it all. I willed myself to keep it together, to just keep moving until I was safely inside. Reaching the back porch, I remembered my keys were still somewhere in the bottom of my purse. In the early winter night, the porch was blackened. The porch light, always flipped on, must have been shut off by the thoughtful policemen ransacking my house. A sob bubbled up as I desperately clawed through my bag.

"Abby!" I looked across my porch toward Jake's house. "God, Abby, are you all right?"

"I can't find my keys." My voice came out muffled and weak.

"I'll grab a flashlight. I'll be right over." He spoke calmly, gauging my fear.

I slumped onto the bench near the door and waited. The shouting had died down from the front walk now that I was out of sight. Within minutes, he was scooting through the gate between the houses and up the snowy steps.

"Hey, it's okay. I'm here." He sat next to me, gingerly putting his arm around me.

"Oh, Jake." My arms wrapped around his waist. "He's dead, Jake. They think I did it. They have a video of me pushing him off the platform, but it wasn't me." I looked at him beseechingly.

"I know, honey, I've seen the news. Come on, why don't you give me your purse and I'll help you get inside, okay?"

I released my hold on him and shoved my bag

across our laps.

"This isn't a purse, it's a suitcase." He pointed the flashlight inwards and within seconds, had found the keys. My hand shook violently as I reached for them. "No, just tell me which one. I think it's going to take you another ten minutes to get it in the lock. Let's just get inside."

He opened the door, letting me through. When I flicked on the lights, I could see cabinets opened, plates left strewn on the counter. My junk drawer had been upended on the floor. Jake ran ahead to close all the blinds in the front room. "This is a mess. I can't stay here. Maybe my brother Devin can put me up for a few days, until I can get it cleaned up. I'll just go pack a bag and drive over." I paused. "Except I can't drive over. I left my car on the street and it's probably buried under a pile of snow. They'll mob me if I do that. I should have had my dad's driver wait for me."

"Let me help you get things back in place, at least what we can. Then I had an idea. Instead of staying with Devin, even if I sneak you over in my car, the reporters will probably have figured out where all your family lives. I have an empty apartment a few blocks away in one of my buildings. It's unfurnished, but the heat is on. I already took over an inflatable mattress and blankets and pillows, thinking you might need a place to crash. What do you say?"

I peeked through the blinds at the crowd idle on the sidewalk. "Jake, that's so nice of you. I should say no. Getting you involved seems like a bad idea but I couldn't sleep a wink knowing they were out there."

"Great. Why don't you go get your stuff? I'll go start sorting through the mess down here. We can talk about the case and what the police have once we get settled in at the apartment."

Upstairs, in the primary, Jim's shirts were scattered on the floor. I remembered trying to destroy one of those shirts and a wave of guilt hit me. While I hadn't killed him, my hatred toward him had been so strong. Somehow, I had redirected that anger into the world and caused him to fall from the platform.

In his office, sports trophies still lined the shelves untouched. I sifted through the mounds of papers, all legalese. Would there be any scrap of paper that would offer a hint as to the real murderer? I had clearly been set up as the fall guy. It could have been a man or woman in the coat that pushed him. Perhaps there was a clue in the video. They had probably shown part of it on the evening news. I could look for an old clip.

Deep in thought, I packed absentmindedly and went back downstairs. "I'm ready."

Jake popped his head out of the kitchen. "Great, I got a good start cleaning up in here. If you leave me your keys, I'm happy to come over and clean up some more later tonight."

"Jake, I don't know how to thank you and I don't know why you're being so nice to me."

"Abby, we're friends. You're a really nice person and you don't deserve what's happening." He looked at the ground. "Seriously, I just want to help. I can't just sit here doing nothing while you go through this by yourself."

"Thanks, Jake. Let's get out of here." We walked out the back, locked the door, and went quietly through the fence.

He leaned over and whispered in my ear, "There's

definitely been a few guys in the alley. Why don't you get in the back and keep your head down?" We were in his garage. After throwing my bag in the front, he folded the seat back for me to crawl in. It was a tight fit, more comfortable for a child. My wet boots slipped a little climbing up and I felt his reassuring hands, strong and firm around my waist, stabilizing me, grounding me.

I draped myself halfway across the back. Jake opened the garage. There were voices outside, but we passed without incident. The apartment building was a few blocks away. After parking on the street, Jake insisted on carrying my bag up the three floors to the unit.

"Sorry, it's only a studio," he said, unlocking the door. "You can pretend you're in college or something."

"It's perfect. Thanks." It was a small efficiency, with a kitchen on one wall and the door to the bathroom open across from the entrance. A card table with two chairs had been set up near the kitchen counter, with a mattress under the small windows at the front. "Truly, this is lovely."

"Okay, well, you get settled. I'm going to go pick up some food, ok? Sorry. I didn't think about TV or your laptop or anything. I could go back to your place and grab it, if you want?"

"No, I had left it on the dining room table. It wasn't there so I assume the police have it."

"Well, I can bring you my tablet."

"That would be great. I'd like to find the clip of Jim falling off the platform online. I'm assuming they've been playing it on the news. There might be a clue in it."

"I can do better than that. One of my best friends works at the station. I bet he could get me a thumb drive of the video they pulled in its entirety."

"That doesn't seem ethical. Your friend could get into trouble."

"Well, I can ask him. If nothing else, maybe he can offer up some angles on the case the police are looking at. We're like family. He'll want to help."

"Okay, I trust you." I smiled wanly.

Jake left, and I puttered around the small room, pulling out my phone to call my parents and tell them my whereabouts. I didn't want them to send Devin over and then panic when there was no one home.

"Wait, where are you?" My mother exclaimed. I told her for a third time.

"Mom, it's fine. Jake is my neighbor. He owns a few apartment buildings in the neighborhood. I'm using one of his empty units."

"Why have we never heard of him before? You should be home with us. I don't understand why you left in the first place. You're safer here."

"I'll be fine, Mom. I just need to think things through."

"Hold on a second, your father wants to talk to you."

"Are you all right, Abigail?"

"Yes, Dad, I'm fine. Did you hear anything more from the lawyers?"

"Not your defense lawyer, but your wills guy. Jim filed a new will recently. There is nothing about his burial wishes. It's relatively straightforward. He is leaving all his assets to one person."

"Me?"

"No. Little David, to be held in trust with Lee in charge until he reaches the age of twenty-five."

"Really? Jim had talked about setting up a college fund for David. We'd done our wills together after our marriage, putting each other as the beneficiary."

"Well, he must have thought to change it before he filed for divorce, and Eliza Stanton has so much money it would be pointless to leave it to her."

"You're right. I really have no right to be hurt. It is sweet he wanted to see David taken care of."

"David will be well-taken care of. Jim had amassed a tidy little sum."

"Had he? I didn't know that. Our finances were always kept separate."

"Well," my dad began as Jake rapped on the door behind me.

"Dad, thank you, but I have to go."

Hanging up, I was perplexed that Jim would leave everything to David and irrationally hurt that his first priority before leaving me had been to change his will. This involved forethought. How long had he been planning to leave me? Doubtless, the police would consider this even more motive, though the money didn't matter to me. I was hurt by the deception. His kindness to me before Christmas had led me to believe we were growing closer, not pushing apart. He had been assuaging his guilt by buying me trinkets, allowing me one last holiday before he blew up my world.

When I opened the door, Jake was holding a pizza in one hand and some bags with plates and paper towels in the other.

"Here, let me put that on the counter." I took the box so he could extricate himself from the bags.

"There's some diet pop in one bag and a bottle of wine. There's a box of donuts for the morning. I remembered your sweet tooth."

"This is more than fine. I can't thank you enough for helping."

I started to tear up again. Jake tentatively approached me and put a loose arm around my shoulder. My cheek pressed into his soft flannel shirt. His other arm reached around me, cupping the back of my head, softly stroking my hair. "I'm so sorry, Abby. It'll be ok, we'll figure it out."

He continued to murmur reassuring nonsense as I let out my tears. I hadn't had a good cry since coming home yesterday, after the altercation with Jim. Then I had been mourning my marriage and feeling sorry for myself. Today, I was terrified for my freedom and coming to terms with being a widow instead of a divorcee.

"I'm sorry, I'm such a mess." I ripped off a piece of paper towel to wipe the tears from my face.

"I don't mind. You've been through a lot. It's only natural. Let's eat something, okay? You sit down and I'll get it." He placed a slice of pizza on a plate and brought it over. "You need to eat."

The food was tasteless. "I can't believe he's gone. It doesn't seem real."

"You want to tell me what happened? I understand that you're a suspect, but why are the cops so sure you did it?"

"He broke up with me yesterday morning. On his way out the door, like super casual. By the way, our marriage is over. I guess I got mad."

"Wow. I can imagine. Did he say why? You guys looked happy when we saw you a few weeks ago on your way to that black-tie event."

"He'd met someone else. Someone at his firm. I actually saw them together at the party. They were in a corner arguing. I had assumed they were talking about work, but her husband had come up to me and asked me if I was ever jealous. I had thought it was strange at the time, but now, I feel like such an idiot. It had never occurred to me to think he might be working long hours and having an affair."

"Who was she? Had you met her before? Maybe the jealous husband had something to do with it."

"Eliza Stanton, like of the billionaire Stantons."

"Huh, so this was a definite step up socially for him."

My chin jerked up. "What makes you say that? She's a beautiful woman, she's smart. Why is this about his social climbing?"

"He just seems like a guy who evaluates people based on their success. The few times we talked, he'd always been so goddamn condescending. He was flat out rude to some of my friends at that barbeque ages ago, the guys who are just working class stiffs. I mean, Abby, the guy was a total tool."

"He's dead, Jake. That's really unkind."

"The guy left you, Abby, for a better thing. He's an ass. No one deserves to die, but I'm not going to sugarcoat it." Jake rubbed his forehead and sighed. "Let's not fight. I can pull up a news clip of the video on my phone. I don't remember being able to see much of the person's face. Was her husband a big guy?"

"No. Brian is thin. About my height, but I was probably wearing two-inch heels."

"It's possible he could have put on the same coat. But how would he know to follow Jim to the train?"

"Jim took the train every day, no matter the weather. He was neurotic about being on time to work every day. He was always at the platform between nine and nine fifteen."

"This party was like two weeks ago. If the husband had had his suspicions, or maybe even flat out knew but didn't want to rock the boat at the party, he would have had time to plan this. The snowstorm would have been a perfect situation. The streets were empty. The local news had been talking about it well over a week in advance. Most people would have stayed home that day, making it easy to get away. The platform was icy so he wouldn't have even had to give Jim much of a shove. Your husband was a big guy. It makes sense that it was another man."

I was starting to get excited. "Jake, you might be on to something. Maybe we could do some research on him. Brian Everly. He runs his own gallery. There has to be some press about him. Maybe he's in financial trouble. Galleries are never particularly successful. With Jim out of the picture, Eliza could be convinced to stay with him and work through the issues in their marriage. There's no way Brian would have gotten anything in a divorce. Their prenup is probably iron clad."

We watched the video on the tiny screen, pulled from some news article. "Honestly, the only thing you can tell from this video is that the person has lighter skin. The hair is all tucked away, and the scarf is strategically wrapped around their face. The pants could be either gender. I think we have to consider this Everly guy our top suspect."

For a brief second, I allowed myself to hope. "How do we investigate him, though? How do we get the police to take a look at him?"

"Let me talk to my friend and see if there's anything he can do. I would think they would require alibis for anyone tangentially associated with this mess." He paused. "By the way, you never mentioned your own family, except in the most basic of terms."

"What was there to say? I have parents and three siblings, all of which I've mentioned. You've even met one of my brothers."

"Your father is a senator. Your grandfather is a senator. It's kind of a big deal, Abby."

"Not when you grow up with it. It's nice to meet someone who doesn't know that about me. Who knew me as Abigail Hardy only, not Abigal Lethican Hardy."

He took a long look at me. "I like you, Abigail, whatever your last name is. You're right, it shouldn't matter to me as your friend. But in terms of this case, I think it buys you some time. They're going to want to make sure everything is sewed up tight before they officially press charges."

"My father had some defense lawyers up at the house this morning. They said the same thing."

"We have some time to work on an alternate theory. Your lawyers probably use private investigators. We could give them Everly's name. There might also be someone else at work, or a friend or something that could be angry with him? What about that cousin of his? The one with the little boy."

167

"Lee? I don't know. I can try to talk to her. My brother Devin is actually dating her. I was planning on calling her just to check in anyway." I knew I was being too open but it was hard not to feel safe with this man who chose to stay with me and work out the details of the case while protecting me from the reporters. "My dad was on the phone when you knocked. He told me the details of Jim's will. Jim had changed it just last week, before Christmas. When he decided to leave me, he had updated the beneficiary from me to her son, David, for the entirety of his estate."

Jake looked at me, his eyes narrowed. "Isn't that a little weird? His cousin's kid? Does he have any other family?"

"Not really. His dad is still living, but he's in poor health. They are not close and he probably thought he was going to outlive him. His mother and grandmother had both passed. There were no siblings. Lee and Jim had grown up together and were really close. We actually moved up to Lakeview so we could help her once she had a baby. David's dad isn't in the picture, you see."

Jake nodded. "Okay, well, that makes some sense if you think about it. Leave your money to your youngest relative. It could've just been a place holder in his mind. He could have changed the will again if there had been children with this Stanton woman."

"He was so fond of David. He loved him. I'm not really surprised at all by it."

"Well, you must be exhausted. I'm going to let you be. If you think of anything or anyone else, text me. I'll give my buddy on the force a call on my way home."

"I feel so much less alone with you helping me."

Jake put the remaining pizza in the fridge before walking to the door. "I'll see you tomorrow, maybe around ten a.m.?"

"Sure. See you then, and thanks again."

After he left, I looked around the small apartment, feeling antsy. A hot shower might relax me. I undressed, waiting for the water to warm up. My phone rang on the kitchen counter with my mother's signature ring.

I ran out of the bathroom, not thinking to grab a towel. At the same moment, the door opened. I froze. Jake walked in. His sharp inhale filled the room. We stared at each other. "God, you're beautiful." He shook his head and turned around. "I mean, I'm so sorry. I did knock. I just came back to drop off a charger for your phone. I forgot to bring it earlier."

Without speaking, I sprinted back to the bathroom. The apartment door banged shut. The water in the waiting shower was scalding. I relished the heat on my skin, driving out the mortification washing over me. I had been so embarrassed to be caught naked. Jake's eyes, however, had not indicated embarrassment. He had seemed so appreciative, sweeping his gaze over me from top to bottom. Jim had never stared at me with such hunger.

I was too rattled by the encounter to call my mother back, instead texting her my assurance that I was safe in my new lodgings. Tossing and turning on the blow-up mattress, I struggled to get to sleep. It was late in the morning by the time the phone's buzzing woke me. Jake's text said he was on his way with coffee and had something important to talk to me about.

Ten minutes later, I was dressed and ran to open

the door at the first knock. He came in, fairly bursting. "Hey. I thought of something. I need to talk to you about it. First off, I'm really sorry about coming in here like that. I knocked and then the phone rang and I just assumed it was okay to come in. I don't know why. It was not, and I'm sorry."

He paused, looking me over, and waited for my response. My cheeks felt hot. I choked out, "It's fine. It was an accident. What do you have to tell me?"

"Well, it's kind of awkward, on all counts. I spent a lot of last night thinking about you, I mean how you looked." He stared awkwardly at the ground. "I mean, you look amazing. Don't get me wrong, but something was bothering me about the whole thing."

My face scrunched in confusion. "I thought this was something to do with Jim's murder?"

"It is, I mean, it might be. You don't have any tattoos."

"No, God, my parents would have killed me if I got a tattoo. It's a real sticking point with them. My oldest brother got one on spring break in college. I thought the walls of the house were going to fall down with all the shouting. What do tattoos have to do with anything?"

Jake looked around nervously. "It could be nothing. We already know he was having an affair." He took a breath. "One time, I was walking down my gangway and, I don't know why, but I looked up. I could see into the window of that bay, the one by your dining room. It was the back of a man, unclothed. He moved aside and I saw a flash of a naked woman. It was quick, just a few seconds. She had a small cross tattooed on the front of her hip. I remember being shocked at the time that you'd have a tattoo like that.

Maybe a little butterfly, but a cross? It just didn't seem to fit. Anyway, I assumed at the time it was you and it was none of my business anyway."

"Wait, you're saying you saw Jim having sex with someone in my house…in my dining room?"

"I am saying there were two naked people, a man and a woman, in your dining room. There was probably sex involved."

"You're sure it was a cross?"

"Yes, definitely a cross. One of those Celtic ones. It could be Eliza Stanton. I don't think we can call her up to ask about her tattoos."

Shaking my head in agreement, I looked up at him, feeling sick. "It really doesn't seem like something she would do. There has to have been another woman. Eliza is Jewish, there's no way she would put a cross on her body. Oh my God, when was this? How many different women do you think there were?"

"It was early fall. I remember it was still warm out."

"I've been such a fool. I had no idea." My hands covered my face. I had traveled often for work. Did he go out those nights and pick up random women? Had there been multiple mistresses? It explained his lack of interest in our marital bed. He was probably exhausted by the end of the week juggling them.

During the law school years, we'd spent so much time together compared to recent years when he had been working. His claim to be at the office most nights no longer rang true. It didn't matter in the context of his murder, though. I had to move forward. My only focus now was clearing my name.

"What time of day was it?"

"It was still light out. Sometime in the afternoon. Why?"

"It wouldn't have been someone he picked up at a bar then. There has to be another mistress, at least one more. She could also have a jealous husband. Or she could have been angry. Maybe he dumped her and me for Eliza."

Jake nodded as his phone buzzed. "Hey, it's my buddy Mike. I convinced him to come by and share what he knows. Are you willing to talk to him? It's all off the record, though, so you can't bring it up with your lawyers or anything."

"Yes, absolutely. At least I'll know what I'm up against."

Mike arrived shortly after. He was a squarely built guy with a buzz cut. Jake clapped him on the shoulder. "Thanks for coming up, Mikey. This is Abigail. You two met this summer at the barbeque."

"Hey there. I'm sorry about your husband."

"Thanks, and thank you for coming to talk to me. I promise not to mention it to anyone."

"Yeah, I could get into a lot of trouble. This is just a favor to Jake." He looked nervously at his friend. "I have to be honest. It doesn't look good. While I would like to say, since you're Jake's friend and we've met before, you're not really the type to kill her husband, but after working this job for a few years, I've learned anyone can commit a crime of passion."

"Is there anything besides the camera footage from the El?" Jake asked. "The jacket is obviously a match, but there's nothing to indicate if it's a man or a woman from that footage. What about the cameras downstairs in the station when you walk in? Do those show anything?"

"No, that's more of the same. The person who pushed your husband came in with their head low, holding on to the oversized hood of the coat. The best we can make out is that the person has no beard. He or she was wearing what looks like black sweat pants and black boots. Here's where the problem comes in." While he had been talking, he pulled out a laptop and thumb drive. "There's a video of you, clear as day, no hood, same jacket, volunteered by one of your good Samaritan neighbors after the incident. You also appeared to be wearing black pants with black boots. It's clear that you pushed him from behind while he was walking away. This makes you the most likely suspect. You were angry and you had motive. The clarity on these videos is not great, especially with the snowstorm happening, but it's clear enough. Here's the good news. There is one strange thing about the video from the train station. The person who perpetrated the murder actually arrives a few minutes before the deceased. He or she then proceeds to wait on the platform off to the side, facing the wall next to the platform. The suspect would have had a clear view of the stairs from that location. Your husband coming up the stairs, however, would have had to turn around backwards to spot the attacker. The attacker waits until the train is pulling into the station, then pivots and runs full speed at the deceased. The part that was shown on the news is just the clip of the victim being pushed. The attacker lying in wait makes it seem a bit more premeditated."

"I admit to pushing Jim when we were on the street by our house, but I didn't follow him to the train station."

"Without your phone on you, that's a little hard to prove. It takes a lot of coincidence to have a body double show up ten minutes later and kill your cheating husband for you."

His words fell over me like an icy blast as my impending murder charge became real. In the little bubble of my privileged existence, bad things happened to other people. There was never anything so horrible that my father couldn't have fixed as long as I avoided drugs and stayed in school. Every other path would be smoothed over. Now I was facing prison time. Even with the best lawyers, I no longer liked my odds of being proven innocent. "What about Eliza Stanton, the woman with whom he was having an affair? Or her husband?"

Mike took a breath. "About that—the station had Stanton come in for a little chat. Her husband came with her for moral support. They were looking pretty cozy. She seemed shaken up by the whole thing and he was going to be there to pick up the pieces and work himself back onto her good side, if you know what I mean. She had just landed at the airport. She'd been visiting a client out in California. The husband was at home at the time, on a zoom call."

My head pounded. The mystery woman had to be the key to the whole thing. Jake spoke up, coming to the same conclusion. "Mike, I definitely saw him with another woman, naked, through the window at their house a couple of months ago. This guy seemed to make a habit of cheating. The woman's face was not visible. Do you have any ideas on how we could trace her?"

"Not really. Follow the money would be my best guess. There's a chance he was paying the woman. He was a good-looking guy, though. I'm guessing there are quite a few ladies who would do it for free. There's one more thing, and then I have to get going. That cousin of his, the really hot chick?"

"Lee." My response came out in a monotone.

"She came in beside herself. She put up a good show, crying about what a hero Jim was, how supportive he had been to her and her kid. She also claimed Jim had told her at Christmas he was pulling the plug on your marriage because he'd found 'the love of his life'. That's a direct quote. Apparently, Jim was very concerned with your reaction. He thought you were 'obsessed with him', another quote, and might do something drastic. Were you with them at Christmas?"

"Yes, I was there." I paused. "It was at my parents' house. Jim did speak with her. In fact, he made a point of taking her aside to the library. My brother, Devin, who is also Lee's boyfriend, was furious. Devin never liked Jim because Jim was always really controlling with Lee. When Lee came back, she seemed upset. She only stayed for part of dinner and then Devin took them back home."

"Them?"

"Yes, her son was there of course."

"Did you talk to Devin about it afterwards?"

"No, the first I saw or heard from him was when he came to check on me after the police had showed up to tell me about Jim's death. He only lives a few blocks away, in the same building as Lee actually. It's how they ended up dating."

"What's your relationship with Devin like?"

"We're not that close. We always fought as children and then when I started dating Jim, the two of them butted heads constantly. We mainly stayed out of each other's way."

"Do you think Devin might have anything to do with the murder? Lee claims to have not shared Jim's news with Devin, but maybe she's covering up for him. Could he have been angry that Jim was leaving you?"

"You're suggesting my brother framed me for murder?"

"It's a stretch, but we don't have many other leads. You really are the most likely suspect at this point." Mike walked toward the door. "All right, man, I'll call you if I find out anything else."

After he left, Jake came over and put his hand on my shoulder. "Are you okay? That was a lot to process."

"No, I'm not okay. Why would Lee say any of those things? How had I not noticed that my husband has probably been cheating on me for most of our marriage, possibly our whole relationship. I just feel so blindsided." The tears started spilling out. Jake kneeled down in front of my chair.

"I'm really sorry, Abigail. I wish the bastard had just walked out of your life. Or better yet, that you'd never met him at all. I wish you had met me instead."

My eyes grew wide. "What do you mean?"

"Clearly, this is not the time, but I have had feelings for you since the day we met. I tried to put it out of my mind and just be your friend. Obviously, you were married, but the guy was such a jerk, it was hard to watch you guys together. I am going to help you get through this, no matter what, no matter your feelings toward me. I just want to be honest with you and let you know you can depend on me. There has been enough lying in your life."

"What about Nicole? You guys seemed so happy."

"Nicole is great. She's a nice girl. It just wasn't working. I broke it off with her. The night you and Jim went to that party and you were all dressed up, you took my breath away. She didn't have the same effect on me and I didn't want to waste her time."

"Jake, this is so crazy but I felt it too. This is too much to think about right now, but I want you to know that you didn't imagine anything. Your friendship has meant so much to me, more than I was willing to admit to myself."

His eyes sparkled at my declaration. "Okay, I can appreciate that. So, for now, let's table this and figure out how we're going to clear your name. After that, we can talk about our first date. I'm thinking maybe Hawaii for a month? Relaxing on the beach sounds pretty great."

I laughed. "A month long first date? I didn't know you were so romantic."

"I'm usually not. You make me want to be romantic. Now, back to the case. Can you call up Lee and talk to her? Don't mention Mike's involvement in this, but maybe ask her if she had talked to Jim about the divorce or if the cops had spoken to her yet?"

"I can try. Lee has never really liked me. She's always tolerated me, like a stray pet that Jim picked up along the way. She's never very friendly to anyone, unless she's drunk, and then she usually falls all over the nearest interested male. I was surprised she and Devin hit it off. He's kind of a high brow, the great intellectual type. Of course, she's gorgeous, so that helps, but they can't have that much in common. Maybe I should call Devin first, see if she's said anything to him. I need to thank him for coming to the police station with me anyway."

"Okay, text me later. There are some things I need to take care of in the shop. I'll come by with dinner again around six. We'll figure this out," he said, walking to the door.

Alone, I sprang into action, grabbing my phone. Devin answered on the last ring. "Hey, Abigail. I can't really talk, what's up?"

The sharpness of his words surprised me. I was fighting for my life and he was busy? "Sorry to bother you. I just wanted to thank you again for coming to the station with me and see how Lee and David were doing."

His breathing was slow and measured. He took so long to answer I thought he might be about to hang up. "Not great. Lee has been really distraught. Truthfully, she thinks you're the one who killed Jim...that you murdered him in a fit of jealousy."

"What?! That's absurd! I never even hit you back as a kid. I just went and cried to Mom. I'm the least violent of all of us."

"Yeah, but jeez, Abby, I just don't know what to think. The footage they keep playing on the news? It sure looks like you."

"It's not though. I'm being framed. You have to tell me. Did she say anything else?"

"She's been crazy, really, all over the place. She's hyper one minute, sobbing the next. She wants me to marry her and take her far away so she can forget all of it ever happened."

"Marriage? You guys have only been dating a few months. The solution to her trauma is to marry the brother of the woman who killed her cousin?"

"Well, she's not thinking clearly. Honestly, before this happened, I was considering breaking up with her. She always runs so hot and cold with me. I had hoped the holidays would bring us closer together, that being with the family would change the dynamic. She was always so terrified of what Jim would think. If she felt like she could belong in our family, maybe that wouldn't matter so much?"

"Did she talk to you about their conversation in the library that day?"

"No, she told me to drop it. We barely talked at all the drive home. I left her and David at their front door that night. We didn't have any contact for a few days, then the accident happened. I had thought she needed space, and I was fed up with the whole situation. There was a part of me that hoped she would think the relationship had run its course and break up with me. Now, I feel like she's so crazy, I can't leave."

"Do you think she'd talk to me?"

"Probably not. She'll probably just scream at you."

"Did you know Jim left her his money, in trust, for David?"

"Yeah, she mentioned it, but it's pretty tied up. She can only access it for school basically, and then he gets the remainder on his twenty-fifth birthday. It made her angry Jim thought her too stupid to be in control of the money."

"Interesting. One last thing, Devin. Before you ask if she'll talk to me, can you find out if she thought Jim was seeing anyone else, besides Eliza? Be slick about it so she doesn't think I'm asking and clam up."

"You think he had multiple women on the side?"

"You know my neighbor, Jake, the guy with the furniture store? He saw Jim through my dining room window with someone, you know, in the act, but I don't think it was Eliza and Jake didn't get a good look at her. There might be a jealous husband somewhere."

"Okay, I'll talk to her. I'm sorry I was so short with you. It's just hard to know what to think."

"It's okay. You feel the need to protect both of us. I'll talk to you later."

Chapter 12

My text messages buzzed. It was my father. —*The lawyers want you to come in to the office. It sounds like the DA will be pressing charges tomorrow. They want to prep you. Can you make it downtown in an hour? I will meet you.*—

My hands started shaking. It was happening so fast. There was so little time to consider who else would have framed me. It felt like time was spiraling forward and all I wanted to do was press the pause button. — *Yes, Dad. I'll see you in an hour.*—

I took a deep breath and went through my bag to find clothes that weren't the sweats I had slept in. Once dressed, I called an Uber to go downtown. I kept a mental tally of new information to share with my lawyers. With the DA pressing charges so quickly, the window to clear my name was shrinking. There was no real evidence and what I had was thin. Lee's pronouncement of me as a murderer had been damaging to my psyche. Could she really think I had it in me to brutally slay my own husband? If she felt that way, what chance would I have in front of a jury? They would probably have her testify. I could see the headlines in my mind, "Murdered husband's family proclaims Senator's daughter guilty!"

Feeling tense, I arrived at the lawyers' office and was ushered back immediately by a very polished receptionist. My father had hired the best criminal attorneys in Chicago and the place had an air of quiet money. The expensive furnishings were meant to inspire confidence that this was the best that money could buy. Hopefully, their cumulative expertise would be able to set me free.

I sat down next to my father. He reached out for my hand. Feeling his warmth brought the tears back into my eyes but I pushed them away and tried to focus.

One of my lawyers, a Mr. Abe Gold, looked at me, owl-like through his glasses from across the table, and nodded. "Mrs. Hardy. I was just explaining to your father how the next few days would go. Tomorrow, the DA will be pressing charges. I have already taken the liberty of telling them you would willingly turn yourself in at the appointed time. There was no discussion of a plea deal."

Agitated, I interrupted. "I'm innocent, anyway. I wouldn't take one."

"Of course, of course." Mr. Gold waved his hand as if the question of innocence or guilt were moot in this situation. "The thing is, it tells me they believe they have a strong case, which is not good for us. They also think this trial will be a big splash for the DA's office. You'll be charged tomorrow morning. The DA is planning on a media circus, so make sure you stay calm and collected. I've spoken to the judge for your bail hearing. He wants to get it done and out of the way, so once you've been processed, we'll be going straight into court. You've been cooperative, and there is no reason to the think the DA will insist on no bail. Wear something simple tomorrow and leave your nice jewelry at home. Preferably all black to indicate your mourning. It'll look better for the cameras. We'll worry about our defense later, but I can tell you as of right now, since you have no clear alibi, our best shot will be to sow doubt in the jurors' minds."

Interrupting him, I shared Jake's suspicions that Jim had been cheating with multiple women. Mr. Gold nodded. "That's interesting. It could be an angle, but it's not a lot to go on. He didn't actually see the other woman's face. We'll have the investigator check bars around the neighborhood. You travel a lot for work. It says here you're out of town three to five days a month. Is that right?"

"Yes," I replied, realizing what he was implying.

"Well, that gave your husband plenty of time to be out with another woman and not risk running into you. There's a possibility someone recognized him, or maybe he had a spot he liked to frequent. I'm not going to lie, it's a long shot, but if we can find some proof that he had been cheating with multiple partners, it's another opportunity to instill some doubt.

"The big angle here is that you were pictured on a neighbor's doorbell camera physically pushing the deceased at nine seventeen a.m. We already knew about that per what you had told us, but I don't like that they have it on tape. That is not going to play well. The upshot is, at nine twenty-five, someone wearing the infamous jacket is seen walking in to the train station. The deceased doesn't show up until nine twenty-nine. Now, this is interesting because at nine nineteen, you had just gotten up and are heading out of view of the camera. You're much shorter than the deceased so you would have had to sprint to get there ahead of him. Without a snowstorm raging, it would be possible to cross the block and a half and make it ahead of him, no problem. You're a fit girl. With the snowstorm raging and the sidewalks not yet shoveled, six inches deep with snow, it seems like a stretch. That's the good news. The bad news is you are by far the only suspect with any real motive. We'll look into the idea of another paramour, but it's a little bit of a reach that we will find anything.

"I suggest you go home, relax, have a good meal and be back here at ten a.m. tomorrow. Anything else you want to tell me before you go?"

I briefed him on my call with Devin about Lee and her mental state. He shook his head. "That's not great. She's definitely on the witness list. I read her statement to the police. She seems firm in her conviction that you could have murdered him because you were upset. Do you think she comes off as a credible witness?"

"Yes, I mean, she's a professional woman and a competent single mom. She and Jim were very close. My brother says she has been in an overwrought state since Jim's murder. Realistically, she has no reason to try to pin this on me. She genuinely thinks I did it."

"Okay, let me think on how to handle her. Go home, get some sleep. I'll see you tomorrow."

My father and I went downstairs. "You should come home with me. We'll stop at your house and get some clothes. You're better off with your family right now. Please. Your mother is so upset. She will want to see you before you're taken into custody."

I thought about Jake and our plans for dinner. My dad was right—my family was my top priority. Jake would understand. I felt a bit desolate at the thought of not seeing him tonight, though. "Okay, Dad. You're right. I'll come home with you."

We headed back up to Lakeview in my father's car. My car was still on the street. I asked my dad to let me off before the house so I could park it in the garage. The snow on my windshield had melted and then refrozen. I scraped with all my might and then gave up on doing a good job. It didn't matter. I only had to drive it a block back to the garage. Sitting down in the car, memories of that fateful morning came flooding back. Frustrated, I let my tears out in howls, terrified of being dragged into jail the next morning.

Finally, my nerves calmed down and I slid my car out of the spot. The area around the car was hardly clear, but it was enough that I could get out without damaging the car in front. Pulling into the garage, voices rang through the quiet. In the yard, I saw Jake speaking with my father, shovel in hand. He had come over to clear the light falling of snow from last night. The paths were clear. He had shoveled them after leaving me last night. I felt overwhelmed by this little act of kindness and wholly grateful for his goodness and his faith in me.

"Abby, I've just been getting to know your neighbor here."

"Jake, hi. Yes, Dad, this is the friend who let me stay in one of his apartments when the house was swarmed by reporters."

"It was just sitting there empty. I have a few rental properties around here," Jake said.

"Well, we appreciate your help. I should have insisted she stay with us. This whole situation has been very difficult."

"Thanks for clearing the snow, Jake. I won't be

back to the apartment tonight. I am going to spend the night at my parents' house. We are just here to grab some more clothes." I looked at him intently, willing him to not mention that we had made plans to eat together. In this moment, I wanted to keep our relationship a secret. Nothing had happened but I knew, if I ever got out of this miserable situation, I would reach for this man with all my heart, for kindness and caring instead of ambition and power. "The DA is going to press charges and I've agreed to turn myself in. Hopefully, I'll be out on bail in a day or two. After that, I don't know."

Jake nodded, staring at me silently. His fingers nervously drummed across the shovel handle. "Okay, I'm really sorry. I'll keep an eye on the place and shoot you a text if I hear anything."

I smiled and patted his arm as I walked past, Dad following me into the house. Packing quickly, I checked around the house to make sure everything was in order and put all the mail in my bag to sort through tonight. I would be away for a few days at most, but there was a finality as we left and locked up.

Back at my parents' house, my mother was in full panic mode. "Oh, Abby, how could this happen? That idiot DA can't make this case against you stick."

"Mom, I love you, but you're not making this better."

"I'm sorry. I just feel so helpless."

"I know, Mom. We'll figure it out. There has to be an answer somewhere." I told her about the lawyer's strategy for the case. "I hope it works. He's the best out there. At the same time, it just sucks. If I get acquitted that way, there will always be people who believe I did it and Jim's real killer will still be free. I'm at my wit's end trying to think of who else might have wanted him dead."

"When you are released on bail, I'm going to have your brothers all come over for a family meeting, as well as your grandfather. We need to present a united front on this, both for your father's career and for the public to see that we do not think of you as guilty, not for one second. Tommy is flying in from California tomorrow night."

I drew a breath. During this whole horrible week, I had not thought about my father. He would be going back to Washington soon, with the holidays almost over. Instead of attending fundraisers, he had dropped everything to chauffeur me around to the lawyer's office. If I was convicted, it was unlikely he would be reelected. My shame overwhelmed me.

"I'm sorry, Mom. I'm so, so sorry. This has been so hard on all of you. I want you to know you've been amazing. There was no reason to snap at you just now."

My mother drew me into a hug. "We'll get through this. It's just been bad luck. Why don't you go unpack? We need to discuss a few things for the funeral when you get back down."

We had decided on a cremation and a few simple words said at my parents' church, mainly family but some friends and colleagues as well. My mother had called Jim's father. He said he was heartbroken, but his health would not allow him to travel up for the service. I owed him a call myself. I had completely surrendered to survival mode and had spared so few thoughts for anyone else.

Going upstairs, I took a deep breath and took out

my phone to call Eliza Stanton. If she loved Jim enough to leave her husband, she might want the opportunity to say goodbye to him. She answered immediately, catching me off-guard.

"What the hell do you want, Abigail? You have a lot of nerve calling me."

"I just thought you might want to come to Jim's memorial service. It might give you closure."

"I don't want closure. I want Jim. But you took that all away from me."

"I didn't do it, Eliza. I was extremely upset when he told me that he was having an affair with you, that he was leaving our marriage, but I did not kill him. I don't know who did."

"You expect me to believe that?"

"It's true, but I don't expect anything. I get that I look like the most likely suspect. How long were you guys having an affair?"

"Why would I talk to you about this?"

"There was probably another woman in his life besides you. I'm wondering if she was jealous, or if she had a jealous husband."

"You are saying Jim was cheating on me too? You have a lot of nerve. I have to go."

With that, she hung up. I sighed, deciding to text her the date and location of the service. She would likely never pick up another call from me. I went through my bag, hanging up my clothes so they would look unwrinkled for my arrest tomorrow. It was so silly to worry about my appearance at a time like this, but my parents had always taught me that there was value in how you present yourself to the world. I would do my best to look polished, a grieving widow instead of a disheveled psychopath.

Afterwards, I began sorting through my mail. Besides the usual catalogues and adverts, there was a handwritten envelope with no stamp. Curious, I opened it, hoping it wasn't some sort of death threat. It was a note from Nicole, Jake's ex-girlfriend.

I didn't know whether to reach out to you or if it was even important. The news says you killed your husband. I don't know if it's true or not. Jake has always thought the world of you, so I have to think you wouldn't do something so crazy. I ran into Jake and he gave me a little of the backstory. He said that Jim was having an affair with that socialite. I don't know if that's true or not, but I just thought you should know that your husband used to come into the bar where I work. One time, he was looking out the window and he saw someone he recognized. He paid his tab and walked out. Looking out the window, I clearly saw him making out with a woman in the street. She didn't look anything like that woman the papers say he was having an affair with. She was blond, for one thing. I only saw her for a second when they pulled apart but I would recognize her if I saw her again. I don't know if this helps, but I thought you should know. I didn't realize he was your husband until that night Jake and I ran into you on the street. It's probably not my place to tell you what a cheating scumbag he was, but I hope you find out who killed him.—Nicole

I texted a picture of the note to Jake and waited for a response. A few minutes later, my phone rang.

"Looks like you have more proof of another woman," Jake said. "I'm going to reach out to Nicole and see if she can give me a better description, or maybe just figure out what month this happened. Look, you don't have a doorbell camera, do you? We knew he brought her home at least once. If we could go through the old footage, the mystery woman might be on there, assuming they went through the front door."

"No, Jim was really weird about his privacy. He said those cameras were intrusive and a way for tech companies to own us. He was probably just worried about getting caught cheating. You don't mind reaching out to Nicole? I know it can be weird with exes."

"We parted amicably even if we're not really friends. She's a good person who clearly wants to help." There was a pause. "Are you still there?" Jake asked.

"Yes, I just…I'm so scared and I don't know what's real anymore."

"You'll get through this. I'll talk to Mikey. Maybe he has an idea how we can find this other woman."

"What if she doesn't want to be found? What if it was a weeklong affair or there are there are multiple women? We have so little to go on."

"Just stay calm. Listen, a customer just came in. I'm here for you. Call me if you think of anything. Good luck tomorrow."

Later that night, I sat on the couch trying to get into a silly rom-com with my mother. If only life was so simple, a series of mishaps that set you up for life with the perfect partner. There had been no real mishaps in my relationship with Jim, just smooth sailing. Perhaps that's why it had failed. There was no fight in the relationship, nothing to indicate the overwhelming desire of both parties to be together.

My mother was smoothing the blanket over both of

us. "Oh sweetheart, I am so sorry about everything. I had no idea you and Jim were having problems. You'd seemed fine at Christmas. You could have come to me. I know your father and I are often busy with all the responsibilities that come from his work, but we always have time for you. I *always* have time for you. It's hard not to want to come off as perfect in this family. And I know your father and I have a better marriage than a lot of people, but that doesn't mean I can't empathize and listen."

"Oh, Mom, I didn't see it coming. I mean, did we have a perfect marriage? No, but nothing in particular had changed recently. Honestly, in the few days leading up to Christmas, we'd spent some real quality time together. It was the best it's been in a long time." I brushed the hair away from my face and looked up. "It just felt like we were working toward a better future. I didn't know he was cheating on me. He was so busy with his work and I wanted to prove myself as a patient and supportive wife. Apparently, my best wasn't enough so, he went elsewhere." My defeat felt absolute. "In retrospect, I shouldn't have followed him out the door when he broke up with me. I had finally seen him for what he was. I was just angry that I had invested so much time in him, making him into a better man than he was. Five minutes later, I would have cooled off and realized he was giving me a gift, a chance to start over, potentially with someone who wanted me, just for me Abigail, not for Senator Lethican's daughter. It has taken me so long to untwine those two identities, it's hard for me to separate them sometimes."

My mother pulled me into an embrace. "You will have your new beginning. Your father says the lawyers sound upbeat."

"But I will forever be stained with this, even if acquitted. Without knowing the truth of who killed him, people will always be whispering behind my back. It will surely kill Dad's chances at another Senate run. The donors have probably been turning tail already."

"I admit, it hasn't been good. His office has been getting a lot of disapproving calls. He's tried to keep it from you, but you understand the implications. That being said, we love you. You chose none of this. Your father has accomplished a lot in the past few years. He is proud of the work he's done. Retirement may not have been his first choice right now, but he will continue to make a difference in the world, either way, just in a different role."

"Oh, Mom, I couldn't have asked for better parents. I love you."

"We love you too. Now, you should go up and get some rest. Tomorrow is going to be a long day."

Chapter 13

The next day, I was taken into custody. My parents had come with me, the three of us floundering in unfamiliar territory. The media was out in full force as I ascended the steps to the Cook County jail adjacent to the courthouse. The same police officer that had interviewed me read me my rights and took me back for processing. From what I could gather, this was the routine part. My lawyer was inside, waiting. Exhausted from the past few days, a comforting numbness took hold of my emotions. Like a rag doll, I let myself be manipulated by the woman pressing my fingerprints slick with ink onto the piece of paper and mechanically signed anything put before me.

The bail hearing went quickly. The figure was set at a shocking million dollars. My parents had been moving around assets the past few days to have ready cash. Yet again, I was grateful for my privilege and the temporary freedom it would grant me. The next few hours passed in a blur and I suddenly found myself being ushered past the blinking cameras into a waiting car that would drive me back to the home of my advantaged youth.

My brothers were all waiting in the living room. My oldest brother, Will, was closest to the door. He stood up to greet me but it was my youngest brother, Tommy, who came diving across the room to swoop me up in a hug. "Oh, Abby. I flew out as soon as I could. This can't be happening. Jim is not worth it."

I froze, stung by his words. "What is that supposed to mean?"

"The guy has always been an ass. Even in his death, he's still tormenting you."

Will spoke up. "I don't think that's appropriate, Tommy. He was her husband and she's grieving."

"Did you really feel that way about him, Tommy?" I asked.

"I'm sorry, I shouldn't have said anything. We all just wanted the best for you and you seemed to think that was Jim. So we supported you. He didn't deserve to die, but you don't deserve to have your life upended because of him."

"Did you all feel that way? I mean, Devin, obviously you were not Jim's biggest fan." Devin sat across the room and had yet to get up to greet me. He did not look up. "But you too, Will?"

"I tolerated him for your sake. If they weren't accusing you of the murder, I would say good riddance. He was a jerk to you and to Lee, who might arguably have been the only person I've ever met that liked him. My buddy from law school used to work with him. Supposedly, Jim was about as conniving and backstabbing as you can get."

"Then why did you guys let me marry him?"

Tommy looked down sheepishly. "I don't know. We thought you'd figure it out. It seemed like you guys were going to break up for a while a couple of years ago and then all of a sudden you were getting married. Besides, you were pretty pissed off at Devin when he said anything, and we just didn't want you to feel like we were all ganging up on you. It was your mistake to make."

"Let me know if you want me to tell you I told you so," Devin smirked from his place on the couch.

Though he was being sarcastic, it was a relief to see that Devin had come to support me. He had been so strange on the phone a few days ago. Hopefully, it meant he believed in my innocence, despite Lee's accusations.

"Well, I'm definitely free of him now. Now we need to find out who actually killed him in time. Devin, have you talked to Lee at all?"

"I've talked to her a lot. She's still being really weird. She is convinced you killed him. Whenever I suggest anything different, she goes berserk."

"Do you still think I did it?"

"Wait, what?" Tommy looked visibly angry. "You can't possibly think Abigail killed him? She's your sister."

Devin looked at the floor. "I just didn't know what to think. There doesn't seem to be anyone else with motive, and Lee was so sure that your jealousy could have caused you to lash out. But honestly, in my heart, no. I don't believe it. It's all just so crazy."

"Did you ask her if he was having any other affairs? My neighbor, Jake, his ex works at a bar near our house. She saw Jim making out with another woman, a blonde, so it couldn't have been Eliza. There was definitely someone else, but there is no way to tell how serious it was or when it ended."

"She shut me down every time I tried to bring it up. There are a lot of blonde women in Lakeview, Abby. That's not a lot to go on."

"Well, there's one more detail, but I don't know how helpful it is. My neighbor, he was walking past the house down the gangway and he looked up to see two people in a compromising position. He didn't think anything of it. He thought it was Jim and I, but he noticed the woman had a tattoo of a cross on her hip, you know, those Celtic ones with the circle."

"So basically, you need us to ask every attractive blond woman in Lakeview to strip?" Tommy asked. "Perfect, I volunteer to help you."

"Very funny. I know it's not very useful. Devin, do you have any thoughts on it?"

Across the room, Devin sat very still, not making eye contact. "I agree with Tommy. That's a tough lead to follow up on."

We heard a knock at the front door and Will went to open it. "Grandfather! Come in. We haven't started yet." My parents came out of the study across the hall.

"Father, glad you could come. Shall we get started?" We all walked into the living room and sat down. My dad continued, "I've got some ideas that could help. It would be beneficial if Abby and I sat down for an interview with a local news reporter. It could garner a lot of sympathy if we set the right tone. We need to signal our belief in Abigail's innocence."

Devin stood up at the back of the room. "Sorry, I have to go…a work thing I forgot to finish." He came toward me and gave me a hug. "I'm with you, Abigail. I'm sorry I gave you cause to doubt that."

My mother stood up. "You can't possibly be going now, Devin. This is serious. We are having a family meeting. Your sister's life is at stake."

"It can't be helped. I'm sorry." With that, he

hurried out the front door.

My mother, furious, looked at my father. "You can't let him leave like that."

"I'm disappointed he doesn't want to stay but if he's not going to be of any help, what good would it do to force him?"

"It's fine. Dad's right, he won't be able to help. He just feels a lot of guilt about choosing sides, being so tangled up with Lee." My wedding ring caught the light. I wanted to rip it off and throw it away but the optics of going ringless would be noticed by the press. It would stay on until after the trial. After that, I vowed never to worry about optics again and just stay true to myself. "Lee is really upset. She believes I did it. I don't blame him for not wanting to stay."

My phone buzzed in my pocket. It was from Jake.

—*Talked to Nicole. She saw Jim the week after Thanksgiving. It was the same day they decorated the bar for Christmas and she was still busy putting up tinsel when she saw Jim walk out to meet that other woman.*—

My thoughts were racing. If it was the week after Thanksgiving, that was only a few weeks before he had left me. I had been in New York most of that week for work, checking in with clients before the buzz of the holidays had filled everyone's schedules. The affair with Eliza had to have been longer than a month if Eliza had been willing to leave her husband. He had been cheating on both of us.

I opened my text messages again and texted Eliza.
—*I know you're upset, but I really hope you come to the memorial service the day after tomorrow. We need to speak in person. It's important.*—

My father was saying something to me. I looked up. "Sorry I'm so distracted. Whatever you think is best with the interview. I trust you to pick the journalist."

"Okay, Abby, I'll take care of it. It will probably be tomorrow. Why don't you head upstairs to rest for a bit? This has been a lot for you and you probably didn't get much sleep last night. We'll keep brainstorming down here."

Gratitude for my family's kindness overwhelmed me. "Thank you all. I appreciate it more than you can imagine. I think I will go up and rest a while."

Upstairs in my room, I lay down, picking up my phone to see if Eliza had responded. Impatiently, I started thumbing through my news feed, looking for more articles about Jim's murder. There were many headlines about the top 50 songs this year or the best movies of the year. It hit me that tonight was New Year's Eve. Last year, my friend Lucy had been in town and, with Jim, we had gone to a party at a neighbor's place downtown. Jim had been laughing, exclaiming his luck at having a lady on each arm. I had thought we had been happy. Even Lucy had said we seemed to be in a really good place. We had talked to Lucy about house hunting and our intent to start a family after the wedding. Something must have changed in this past year, definitely after we had moved. Perhaps he'd met his unknown mistress in the neighborhood? Eliza had also started working at his firm in the spring. Hopefully, she would come to the memorial. If I could get a timeline on their affair, I could figure out what I had done wrong in my marriage.

Anger ran through me. The blame should not be on my head. Why would he have picked me if I was never enough? Devin's voice rang in my head. "You know why, it's your famous family. For God's sake, Dad even got him into law school and put in a good word for him at the most prestigious law firm in Chicago. Do you think he would have gotten there without you?"

Devin had been right all along. I hoped we could repair the rift between us first caused by Jim and now Lee. There would be no chance to repair anything if I was in prison. My singular aloneness felt like a vise around my heart, despite the presence of my stalwart family downstairs. I texted Jake back.

—*Thanks for the update. If she thinks of anything else, even if she doesn't think it's important, can you have her reach out to me?*—

I paused, thinking about his face when we had been at his rental unit. There had been a look of genuine care and compassion in his green eyes. I felt an overwhelming desire to throw myself into his arms, to be held close. Shame filled me. Were my feelings so cheap I could transfer them from one man to another so quickly? It wasn't sudden, though. We were friends who were attracted to each other, long before Jake's declaration. We just hadn't acted on it, unlike Jim. Unbeknownst to me, my marriage had been over for months. I owed Jim no guilt. My only obligation was to find his killer and move on with my life.

—*I miss you....Happy New Year! I hope you are out enjoying yourself.*—

Nervously, I waited for the bouncing dots, hoping Jake would respond right away.

—*I miss you too. I wish there was more I could do for you. When will you be back in the city? Just going to grab some drinks with friends down the block. Let me know if you need anything, and I mean anything, ok? I really want to be there for you.—*

Without giving it too much thought, I started texting back. *—Would you come to the memorial? It's on the second at noon. I'll send you a link to the address of the church. It would mean a lot to me.—*

—Absolutely. I'll see you then. Have a good night, Abby.—

It would be nice to have someone outside of my family there and I knew my parents were curious about the man who let me stay at his place. There was a knock at my door.

"Come in," I called.

My brother, Tommy, came in. "Hey, Abby, it's dinner time. Mom has been cooking up a storm. She can't sit still."

"Oh yeah? Let me guess, lasagna?"

"How did you guess? Her favorite comfort food."

"I thought I could smell it, and honestly, I was hoping it was lasagna."

He sat down on my bed. "Will is going to head out soon. Apparently, Carol is in the early stages of pregnancy and not feeling very well. He wants to say bye."

"Wait, what? Why didn't anyone tell me?"

"Well, you seem to have a lot on your plate. I think somewhere between your husband's murder and your bail hearing, they must have thought the timing a little inappropriate."

"You're right. I would have kept it from me too. What a mess."

"I'm sorry that this is happening to you. Also, I just want you to know you're my favorite sister."

I groaned at the old joke. "I'm your only sister."

"Finally, something uncomplicated in your life." He kissed the top of my head. "Do you want to talk about it?"

"I don't know what to say. Jim is dead and I don't feel all that sad, which feels horrible. Maybe I'm just so emotionally wrecked from the past few days. Who am I even saying goodbye to? He clearly wasn't the man we all thought he was. The man was cheating on his mistress, for God's sake."

"Well, I've never really trusted him. Remember that time he got drunk years ago, going on and on about that other chick? It was that Thanksgiving you brought him home for the first time. First, he spent the whole time sucking up to Dad and Grandpa, then Devin got him wasted and he couldn't stop talking about some other girl. He was the worst, Abby."

"You said it was no big deal at the time."

"He did catch himself at the time, but if he was still fantasizing about her like that, he couldn't have been that into you."

"Why didn't any of you say anything back then?"

My brother sighed. "I don't know. Now I wish we had. Before Jim and you flew down, Mom read us the riot act about not giving you a hard time. She said this was the first boy you had brought home and we were all to be on our best behavior. Obviously, Devin was still awful, but that's to be expected. We just wanted to support you, I guess. Will and I talked it over and we figured we would let you enjoy yourself. No one thought it was going to last as long as it did. The guy treated you like a doormat. And it's not like you didn't know what a functioning relationship should look like.

You've been surrounded by them your whole life. We thought you were going to figure it out. Maybe you were taken in by his looks? I just don't know. I'm sorry."

My mind was reeling with the eerie sense that I had been living in an alternate universe the past few years. Nothing I thought had been true. "It wasn't so much his looks as his confidence. He could be so engaging. When he wanted to make me feel special, it was magical. And in some ways, I thought he needed me. He was so smart, and so strong, but he still needed me in a way. You guys have always loved me, and for that I'm grateful, but I'm always just the little sister, the tagalong. No one depended on me."

Tommy smiled gently. "We always needed you. You were the kind one. By letting us take care of you, you brought us dumb numbskulls together. You were the peacemaker. Remember all the fights you would get in the middle of? You were fearless. You would just waltz in between the punches flying, knowing we would stop so we wouldn't hit you. God, Abby, I hope this all gets resolved soon. I feel so helpless knowing I can't get you out of this."

"The lawyers Dad hired are really good. My job at the bank is probably done, though. I've been put on temporary leave. If the trial goes my way, I'll probably get out of Chicago and travel for a while. This has all been so horrible. If I'm acquitted, I'm going to start caring only about me. I want to be selfish and irresponsible and find myself, without being Jim's wife, or worrying about his career."

"That makes a lot of sense. You'll get there. No jury could ever believe you did it. We better head down before Mom has a fit and burns the lasagna."

Chapter 14

In the morning, my father came up to my room early. "Are you awake?"

"Yeah, come in. I was just looking at the news on my phone. What's up?"

"The news team will be here at 10 am. We will film in the library." He sat down on the edge of the bed. "This is a stressful situation but I will be right there with you. We're going to keep our answers short. You need to emphasize that you loved Jim and would never do anything to hurt him. The lawyers think we should say something to the effect that you and Jim had grown apart and that his suggestion of divorce did not come as a surprise. What do you think?"

"It's not true, though. I don't want to lie. People saw us together. We looked happy at his holiday party a few weeks ago. He was here for Christmas."

"You could always say you had planned to get through the holidays and then discuss the status of your marriage. It's not uncommon. It's also somewhat true. You've been complaining to your mother about his frequent absences for work. Growing apart can be a natural outcome of that."

"Let me think about it, Dad. The news made sure everyone knew we were fighting right before his accident. Don't you think it will sound a little phony if I say I knew it was coming?"

"Well, maybe not that you knew, but you had been concerned about the relationship. Anyway, I don't know what other questions Lauren is going to have, but she's always been a straight shooter. Now, your mother had your black sheath dress dry-cleaned. It's in your closet. There's a black twinset and skirt for the memorial tomorrow."

"Did Mom tell you to tell me all that? Or do you actually know what a sheath dress is?"

"Your mother, obviously. She's currently busy dusting every square inch of the library shelves. She made me repeat it twice."

I smiled. "I love you. I'll keep my responses short and look properly grief-stricken. I haven't slept through the night since this happened, so the shadows under my eyes should be quite effective at demonstrating my distress."

My father stood up and kissed my forehead. "I'll see you downstairs soon, Abigail-Nightingale."

Taking my beauty arsenal into the bathroom with me, I started to get ready. My stomach felt like a bundle of nerves. This was just the prelude to the trial. It wasn't really even about me. It was about stemming the fallout to my father's career. If I could focus on my dad, instead of my own plight, it might be easier to keep it together.

A few minutes to ten, I made my way downstairs in the plain black dress and minimal makeup and jewelry. My hair was swept back off my face with clips. In the library, a crew was already setting up. My mother came out of the kitchen. "Abby, I didn't want to bother you. Why didn't you come down and get something to eat first before getting dressed?"

205

"I'm too nervous, Mom, or just full from that second helping of lasagna you forced on me. Where's Tommy?"

"I sent him out to run some errands. He was pacing around here, driving me batty. He looks more nervous than you. After you do the interview, we have to call the priest. He wants to go over his eulogy for tomorrow."

"Is there coffee?" My mother went over and poured me a cup. I smiled gratefully, taking it with me to the library.

My father was seated and being mic'd up. Lauren Rivera came toward me and offered her hand. "I'm really sorry for your loss. Thank you for picking me for the exclusive. I promise to be a fair and impartial interviewer."

"Thank you for coming on such short notice. It's been a very difficult time." The tech crew took care of a few last-minute things and we sat down to begin the interview. After a brief review of the murder, Lauren leaned into me with a conspiratorial look on her face. 'Here we go' I thought.

"How long had you known your marriage was on the rocks?"

I inhaled slowly and focused my thoughts. "We had our ups and downs, like any marriage. Jim had been working a lot the past year. He had a very promising career as an attorney and took it very seriously. It's true we did not spend a lot of time together, but I loved him and would never hurt him."

"Is it true that the morning of his death, after he announced his intention to divorce you, you became angry and violent?"

"My reaction was not violent. I was simply upset. I did NOT kill my husband."

Lauren grabbed the remote on the table. I had not taken note of the TV screen placed next to her. "Is it true that you have been extremely controlling in your marriage, pushing your husband in his career and refusing him contact with his own family because you were embarrassed by your husband's humble beginnings?"

"No, I was not controlling!" I felt my dad's hand pat mine, a warning that I was getting too worked up. "Jim was a brilliant man who came from modest circumstances. That is true. I was proud of what he had accomplished."

"We interviewed his family down in Tennessee. Here's what they said." She flicked on the TV. Jim's father was on the screen with the woman he had called his mother in his high school graduation photo. Lauren continued. "Here are Jim's father and aunt, and they claim they have had minimal contact with Jim since he started dating you six years ago." She pressed play.

"My name is Mary, I'm Jim's aunt. We are just devastated at what happened, but not surprised. That wife of his has always been conniving. She just had to get her way. He hasn't been back to see us since he graduated. We weren't invited to their fancy Chicago wedding. He only called once or twice a year."

His father was nodding along to her words. "It's true. Jim's mother passed away from a drug overdose when he was little. His mom and I both had problems with drugs. You know, those opioids. I was injured at work and that's when it all began. After his mom died, I had my wake-up call and I got clean. Jim was a good son until he met that woman. He got a full ride to Vanderbilt, and any extra money he earned working, he would send it home. Once he met up with that fancy senator's daughter, he stopped coming around, stopped sending any money home. Mary here was real hurt. She raised him like he was her own after her sister died. And then he just disappeared out of our lives."

I gulped. What had been a pat on my hand had turned into a viselike squeeze as my father willed me to keep my emotions in check. The video had stopped. My father spoke up before I could. "Abby is a kind and wonderful person. She would never keep Jim from his family. My wife and I believe in Abby's innocence. Thank you so much for coming and letting us express that with your viewers." He stood up, signaling the interview was over.

Lauren eyed him warily, deciding her next move. She capitulated and stood up to shake his hand and then mine. The interview was over. I rushed from the room into the kitchen where my mother was waiting. "Abby! What happened? It can't be over already."

My dad followed me in. "They are packing up to leave. Are you okay?"

"Dad, I have no idea why they would say that. Jim never wanted me to have a relationship with his family. He always said his father wasn't interested."

"What about the aunt? Did he ever talk about her?"

"No! In fact, unless they were twins, the one picture he had of her, he said she was his mom. He told us his mother had seen him graduate right before she passed away from breast cancer, not that she died of a drug overdose when he was a child."

"That's true, John. I remember when he told us

about his mother. Do you remember? It was that first Thanksgiving. Lisa mentioned her mother's passing," my mother's voice hitched a bit, remembering her sister's death. "Jim said he understood because the same had happened to his mother. Oh dear. Why would he lie about such a thing?"

I put my head in my hands. "He was so embarrassed of his background and so, so nervous to meet you. He had never been in such a nice house. He was even impressed with Mom's car. I guess he didn't want you guys to think less of him. College must have been his chance to break free of his past. It couldn't have been an easy childhood. He didn't realize we would respect him more for the adversity he had faced."

"I'm sorry, Abby, the interview was a mistake. It was foolish of me to think I could control the situation. I'm going to see the news crew out and call your lawyers to warn them."

My mom came and sat next to me. "It's awful to find out so many lies at once, Abby. They had a video with his aunt? What did she say?"

"They interviewed his aunt and his dad. They said I was a monster who forced Jim to break contact with his family. Our family was just too fancy to accept them. I just don't know how much more of this I can take. Every day brings some new information and none of it is positive. It feels like every step is the wrong one. What if his family comes up to testify against me? It's their word against mine, but they have nothing to gain and I do. It's going to look terrible." I started crying again. "How stupid am I? Everything that came out of his mouth was a lie. He lied about his family, he lied about being at work, he lied to his mistress. I didn't see any of it."

"Oh, baby. We'll get through this. You just have to have faith."

"I'm all out of faith, Mom. This is me hitting rock bottom."

We sat there for a long time, my mother rocking me back and forth, my tears soaking into her shoulder. Tommy came in through the side door, carrying groceries. "What happened now?" My mother filled him in.

"I'm going to go change and go for a run. We're not talking with Father Ryan for a while, right?" I wiped at my runny nose.

"Yes, you have time. That's a good idea. Why don't you go with her, Tommy?"

He looked over. "I'm happy to come. Can I? We'll just run, like we used to. No talking, just running."

"Sure, I'll see you in ten."

We ran fast; me trying to drive out all the thoughts swimming in my head. Again, I found myself wanting to be with Jake, to tell him what happened and have him hold me. Would he think me a fool for being so taken in by Jim's lie? No wonder my husband had had so little respect for me. Eliza was my opposite, so smart and strong. I felt so small and stupid.

After the run, it was time for the call with the priest. My mother had her laptop open and I sat next to her. Father Ryan had married us almost a year before. He was a kind man who had been at our local parish since my teen years. He spoke his condolences in his lilting Irish brogue and for the first time, I felt only anger, not sadness. It was Jim's lies that had gotten me into this mess. I stood abruptly.

"I'm sorry, Father Ryan. Whatever you think is appropriate to say is fine with me. Mom?" I looked over. "Do you mind handling this? I need some time to myself."

"Of course, sweetheart. Why don't you go upstairs and rest?"

I stormed up the stairs, feeling petulant. I tried to read but couldn't focus. My mother brought a tray of food up for dinner, but didn't push conversation on me. By ten p.m. I was fed up with the thoughts racing through my brain. It was time I focused on my future. I texted Jake.

—*What are you doing? Can I come over?*—

He responded immediately. —*Yes, are you home?*—

—*I'm in Winnetka. I'll be there in 40 minutes.*—

I sprinted downstairs. "Mom, do you mind if I take your car to go back to Lakeview? I'll bring it back tomorrow before the memorial."

"Well, of course you can, but are you sure you want to be alone? It's probably better for you to stay here in case anything comes up."

"I need to get out of here. I appreciate everything you guys have tried to do for me. I just need a little space right now. All the sitting and waiting is driving me insane."

"Okay, Abby. Just don't do anything rash."

"I won't. Love you."

I grabbed her keys off the hook and headed to the garage. I made good time driving down Sheridan Road; the streets deserted at this late hour. Luck was still on my side when I found an empty parking spot down the street from my house. The hood was pulled tight around my face so no one would recognize me. I briefly thought about going back to my house and decided against it. I might never go back, just sell it and move on. It would be easy enough to get movers to handle everything. Ruefully, it occurred to me I might want to get a short-term lease next, in case the state forced other accommodations on me.

I hurried down the gangway of Jake's house, eager to get out of the lamplight of the street and knocked on his kitchen door.

"Hang on," he called through the door.

Just hang on. It could be my life slogan right now.

The door opened. Jake's hair was down from his usual man bun. It was wavy and made him look wild, like a swashbuckling pirate. He ushered me into the house. I went in and stopped very close to him.

"Did you mean what you said?" I whispered, not stepping back.

His eyes stared intently. "About my feelings for you? Abby, of course I did. I'm crazy about you." He reached out one hand and gently stroked my cheek.

"Then kiss me."

"Are you sure, Abby? I'm happy to wait as long as you need. You have a lot going on right now."

"If you care about me, just kiss me. Make me forget everything, just for a little bit."

He didn't hesitate. The hand that had been stroking my cheek opened palm up to cup my face, and he placed the gentlest of kisses on my parted lips. He began slowly and something sparked between us. The kisses grew deeper. Soon we were embracing. At some point, we had stumbled out of the kitchen and down the hall into his bedroom. Within minutes, we were both naked, entwined on the bed. The passion between us was a revelation. My mind slipped away and I let myself succumb to his gentle but urgent body.

When it was over, we both lay there, panting. He had rolled off me but held me close. "Abby," he murmured, making my name sound like an endearment. "Does it make me a creep to tell you that I have thought about this moment a lot and it was even better than I expected?"

"That was pretty incredible. Thank you."

"Thank you? You're not going to leave money on the nightstand and go now, are you?"

"No!" I laughed. "Thank you for everything. You've been amazing and this was amazing and it just feels like it's the only positive that has come out of all of this. Just thank you for being you."

"Okay, better. Thank you for coming over and letting me show you how I feel." He was gently stroking my shoulder, pulling up the covers with his free hand. I closed my eyes and listened to his breathing. For the first time in a long time, the feeling of safety and warmth came over me.

Keeping my eyes closed, I was suddenly desperate for affirmation. "Jim told me once sleeping with me was like sleeping with a bag of hangers."

"That's horrible. He said that to you?"

"I think he preferred curvier women." My response came out as a whisper, my embarrassment acute.

"Abby, as far as I'm concerned, you are curved in all the right places." He tightened his arms around me and burrowed his head in the pillow next to me.

The harsh morning sunlight woke me. Neither of us had thought to draw the blinds. I had fallen asleep and slept through the night, something that hadn't happened since Jim's death. Jake had shifted in the night, but his arm was still arm draped around my middle. I looked at his sleeping form, waiting for the guilt to hit me but it didn't come. My spontaneous decision to pursue Jake had released more than tension. Being with Jake had released me from my husband's shadow. I felt whole.

I looked over at the clock and tried lifting his arm. "Hey you."

"Mmmmm…" Jake muttered and squeezed me tighter.

"I need to get up and get ready for the memorial."

"Right. The memorial." He leaned over and kissed me lingeringly. "Do you want me to come with you now or meet you there?"

"You should come alone and for propriety's sake, we should probably not act like a couple."

"So, do or don't kiss your girlfriend at her husband's funeral? Maybe I should be taking notes."

"Very funny. You're going to make me start feeling bad about what happened."

"I'm sorry. It was a bad joke. I will just be there as your friend. I'll save the kissing for later tonight." He looked up at me with those green eyes of his, the flecks of hazel dancing in the light. "Assuming you would like to come back tonight, of course."

"I'll be here, Jake." I kissed him one last time and started to look around for my strewn clothes. "I feel like I'm on a treasure hunt. When exactly did we start getting undressed?"

"We definitely started in the kitchen. I'll go find your shirt." He threw on some boxers, unashamed in my presence and strode down the hall.

Quickly, I scooped up my things from the bedroom floor and proceeded to get dressed. Jake walked in as I was buttoning my pants. "A guy could get used to seeing this every morning."

"My shirt, if you please, sir."

"I'll trade you for a kiss." He leaned in, handing me the shirt. "Do you want some coffee before you go?"

"I'll grab some on the way. It's getting late."

"Sounds good. And, Abby, I know it's too soon, and I should probably keep this to myself, but I love you." He looked at me, fragile for a second, wondering if he'd overstepped. "You don't need to say anything. I just need you to understand that you are worthy of love and that you are the most attractive woman in the world, to me at least."

For the first time this week, it was happy tears that sprang into my eyes. "Oh, Jake. That means so much to me. You'll never know how much." I kissed him again and hurried toward the kitchen to grab my coat before I started bawling again. "See you at noon, okay?"

"I'll be there."

Chapter 15

I found my car on the street and headed north. My head in the clouds, I may have demonstrated my questionable driving skills with one too many taps on the bumpers of the surrounding cars getting out of the tight spot. It had felt so natural last night to share myself in such an intimate way with Jake. He had made me feel beautiful and desired. Jim had always found me wanting. It was not until I had felt perfection that I knew with conviction how broken our marriage bed had been.

At my parents' house, I found my mother in the kitchen. We would have the few people invited to the memorial over afterwards for snacks and she had thrown herself into the preparation with her usual aplomb. There were trays of canapés and cheese boards covering the large center island. A large vase of lilies graced the kitchen table. The fragrance permeated the house. I had always hated the smell of lilies, associating its sickly sweetness with death, my thoughts drifting back to my aunt's funeral, my young cousin beside herself with loss. It seemed inappropriate to attach that much grief to a smell, especially to that of a beautiful flower.

"Oh, darling, I'm so glad you're back. I don't know what possessed you to spend the night in that house all by yourself. It must hold so many memories for you. Once this is over, you need to let me hire someone to pack up everything and your father will arrange to have the house sold."

And there it was in a nutshell, my gilded existence. Need a job? A friend of dad's will find you one. Murder your husband? Dad will hire the best lawyers. Can't clean up the mess of your life? Mom will hire someone and take care of it for you. When had I stopped wanting to stand on my own two feet? After living in the shadow of my family and Jim for so long, it hadn't occurred to me that I might be my own person. No more. If I was ever free of this murder charge, I would forge my own path and follow my heart.

"I didn't go to my house, actually. I spent the night at Jake's house." I willed my eyes to look my mother directly in the face. I felt like a teenager about to get into trouble for sneaking out with a boy.

"Jake? I don't understand. Is he the nice neighbor who lent you the apartment?"

"Yes, and he's my friend. And he's becoming something more than my friend," I continued awkwardly.

"Honey, you are hurt and looking for comfort, but this just seems too soon. Your husband just passed away. I don't really like the optics of this," she said softly, her tone gentle yet concerned.

"To hell with the optics!" I snapped. "I don't care about the optics. I don't care about how this is going to look. My husband that I'm supposed to be mourning has slept with multiple women in the past few months, and probably throughout our marriage. He treated me like garbage, using me as a stepping stone on his great social climb. I am so sick of thinking about Jim and the position his actions put me in. Jake is an amazing human being that I have come to know in the past year. I trust him, and honestly, he makes me feel smart and funny and beautiful, something that has not happened one goddamn time in my whole charade of a marriage. Besides, if you want to talk about optics, maybe if I move on it will be construed that I didn't actually care about my husband, so why the hell would I have killed him." My words were laced with bitterness.

Concern etched on my mother's face. "Oh, Abby. You have so many emotions right now. The drama of the past week has been overwhelming. If you have feelings for him, and if his feelings are true, they can wait until after the trial. Jim may have been a horrible human being but he was still your husband. You chose him. You should have the decency to mourn him today."

I started to cry, hurt by mother's assessment. "I'm not going to apologize for my behavior. Honestly, Mother, I'm facing prison. There may not be time for a relationship with Jake later. And it was nice to lose myself in his arms for one night and forget about the horror of the last week. I'll be ready in an hour to leave for the church."

I stomped off to my room to get ready for the ordeal ahead. My mother would not make it awkward meeting Jake at the memorial but I felt churlish knowing she would disapprove. My phone pinged. It was the group text I had going with my brothers. Tommy was asking if we were meeting at the house. Will responded before I could, saying we were. I noted that Devin had been absent from the text chain since he had walked out of the house days before. I decided to text him separately. Lee had not responded either to any texts about the memorial. Jim had meant the world to her. I hoped she would feel comfortable enough to show up and pay her respects. I texted Devin.

—*I am assuming you're still coming today. Will Lee be coming with you? I want her to feel welcome. It's a strange situation. I'm happy to keep my distance and give her space.*—

I hit send and waited. Devin usually answered right away. After a minute, I put my phone down to charge. Devin's silence made me nervous, though I couldn't explain why. It hurt me to think he would choose Lee over me, but in a way, I was glad. She had always seemed so alone in the world. There never seemed to be any good friends in her life. She went to work, spent time with David, and occasionally with Jim. Lee had moved up to Chicago without wanting to experience life in a vibrant city.

After an hour, I went back downstairs. Will and Tommy were there. Tommy was asking my dad if he'd heard from Devin.

"No, nothing. I'll give him a call and see if he's on his way." We all milled around as Dad picked up the phone. "No response. Well, maybe he's stuck in traffic. Text him and tell him to meet us at the church. It wouldn't do for us to be late."

We piled into two separate cars. I sat in the back of my brother's car, deciding it would be best to put some space between me and my mother. Her criticism of me had stung.

"You okay back there, Abby?" my brother Tommy asked.

"Fine. I just can't wait for this to be over."

219

"I'm sorry. We'll stand by you when you walk in to shield you from the reporters. Just stay close."

The church was a short ride from the house. There was only one news crew. Hopefully, interest in the story was starting to die down. True to their word, my tall, imposing brothers each grabbed an arm and marched me into the church, their broad shoulders sheltering me from the camera as they both leaned in toward me. Inside, there were a few dozen people. Some of Jim's colleagues sat toward the center and my extended family at the front. Jake had found a place in the back. He gave me a small nod of acknowledgement as I entered but did not come toward us. We swept past all of them to the front pew. Jim's ashes were standing on a table, in a beautiful ornate urn I had not picked out. Of course, it was my mother who had organized this whole day and Jim's cremation with her usual studied grace.

My parents followed in soon after us, stopping to talk with family members on the way. I was impatient to begin the ceremony, the de facto end of my marriage, and move on from the farce of the devastated wife. This week had forced me to grow up. I steeled my face and looked straight at the urn, not making eye contact with anyone. I would be stoic to preserve the appearance of grieving. They would not see me crack.

The priest shuffled in, smiling, and gently took my hand. He bowed over me and gave me a peck on the cheek. "It's God's will, lass. You must believe in Him and His ways. He will see you through this turbulent time."

God's will? Did the priest, with all his good humor, believe his words would be reassuring? God had orchestrated Jim's death in a spectacular fashion to test my faith? It would hardly seem appropriate as far as challenges went. I had crumbled under the weight of it all.

As the priest began his sermon, my mind struggled to focus. Devin had still not arrived. I dared a quick look to see if Lee was somewhere behind me. Eliza made eye contact from the far side of the church. She was immaculately dressed, her back ramrod straight. Her husband sat beside her. His face was appropriately blank, with his arm loosely draped around her shoulder. Perhaps the loss of her lover had forced a reconciliation in her marriage. She nodded at me imperceptibly. I returned the gesture, buoyed by her presence. I would try to speak to her after the service. While obviously there to say goodbye to her lover, her acknowledgement felt like she was absolving me of his murder. It was a small thing, but it gave me the courage to think that others might not find me guilty either.

After a half hour, the priest had finally wrapped up his ministrations. I had listened to so very little of it. He had gone on about marrying us and getting to know us as a couple during that time, and I balked at the recollections being forced on me. Our charming rapport as a couple. It was all falsehood. Jim had been curt during our meetings with the priest, and glued to his phone answering emails. My mind drifted back to Eliza in the back row. Had he been as domineering with her as he had been with me? Eliza was a strong woman. Perhaps she would have been able to keep him in line better than I had.

We stood up as a family to take turns shaking hands with the priest. Some members of my extended family came up to offer condolences. As they moved aside, a few of Jim's colleagues moved forward. Behind them all, Jake was waiting patiently, a soft smile on his face as he looked toward me. I would have to treat him impersonally. My mother was right about the optics, but all I wanted to do was leap into his arms and take off running out the church door.

My closest friend from work was there, Anna, and she came up and pulled me into a hug. "I'm so sorry, Abigail. We miss you at work. I really miss you. No one I've spoken with thinks you could have done this."

She had intended her words to be encouraging, but it struck me how difficult it would be to go back to my life, if I was acquitted. My coworkers had spent hours around the proverbial water cooler discussing my innocence, dissecting little bits of information they had gleaned through the years about my marriage.

"Thanks, Anna, it's kind of you to say and thank you so much for coming." There was a line of people queued behind her. "Talk soon, okay?" I smiled falsely, realizing there was no way I could walk back into my old office again.

Jim's boss approached me. Beside him were Eliza and her husband. Both men shook my hand. His boss, Roger, murmured the requisite, "I'm sorry for your loss. Jim was a hell of a lawyer." Eliza's husband looked awkward standing beside his wife, not knowing whether to make eye contact with his fellow cuckolded spouse. Eliza surprised me by pulling me in for a hug.

"I need to talk to you if you have a minute. Is there somewhere private we can go?"

I pulled away, trying not to get my hopes up. Perhaps she had found some evidence of the other woman? I looked over at Jake and raised my eyebrows, signaling with a shake of my head that he follow us as I guided Eliza away from the crowd. I stopped by Father Mike and whispered, "May I use your office for a private moment?"

"Of course, my child. The door is unlocked. Help yourself."

Eliza led the way in the direction the priest had pointed. We went through the door. When Eliza turned around, she realized Jake had followed us in and closed the door. "Who the hell are you and why are you here?" she said brusquely.

"He's a friend trying to help me piece together clues about who the other woman was. Have you thought of something that might help? If you have, I'd like for Jake to stay."

"If you're uncomfortable with my presence, I can leave. Seriously, Abby, I'll just be outside the door."

"It's fine," Eliza said. "It doesn't matter. You can hear what I have to say." She paused and looked down. "At first, Abby, I thought that you had pushed him, and you know that. But the more I thought about it, I just didn't think you had it in you. You were always such a meek thing. It seemed beyond you to commit such a brutal act of violence."

I winced realizing Eliza found my gentle nature a weakness. "Honestly, Eliza. I didn't kill him. I wish I had waited five more minutes before following him out of the house. I would have realized he was right. Jim and I were not suited to each other. Our marriage had settled into a routine. For what it's worth, I think he really was in love with you."

Eliza's eyes looked glassy with tears. "Thank you.

That actually means a lot to me. I know my husband is here now. Brian and I are trying to work things out, but Jim had become very close to my heart during the past few months."

"When did the affair start?" I asked cautiously, wanting to keep the peace between us, but letting my curiosity get the better of me.

"Last spring. You were out of town on business. We were working on a case. Jim was overwhelmed because you were also in the process of packing up to move. We went out for drinks and ended up back at your old condo. One thing led to another. I'm really sorry, Abby. I've never been a believer in infidelity. This is the first time I've ever cheated. It just became so addicting. The sneaking around, our own little secret, both at the office and at home. Working late and having sex in the copy room when no one was around. For a while it was just hot, you know, and then we really started to fall in love."

I cringed at the visual, imagining them cheating in my own bed. I felt empty from all the deception and my own willful blindness.

"What is it you wanted to talk about? Telling me this serves no purpose." The events of the past few weeks had forced me to grow a backbone.

Eliza nodded. "I was in California when Jim was killed. I had left a few days before for a client meeting. Obviously, I rushed back after hearing of the accident. When I got to my office, it felt like my desk had been rearranged, or searched. Things just weren't in the right place. I would have assumed it was a new office cleaning staff that didn't know I don't like my desk touched, but it seemed like things weren't in the right place in my drawers either. I have a few pictures up in frames around the edge of my bookshelf.

"The other day I dropped a pen and it rolled under the desk. There was a piece of broken glass near the trashcan. I picked it up and put it in the trash, and somehow tipped it over. Under the bin, there was a torn corner of a picture that had been on the shelf behind my desk. I hadn't noticed it was missing until then. It was a picture of me and my father in London from a few years ago. The rest of the picture was gone. What was left was just my face, with a big X over it. I can only assume the glass was from the picture frame being smashed. If it had just been the glass being broken, it could have been a clumsy cleaning person. Crossing out my face made it personal."

"Did anyone dislike you at the firm? Is it possible it's unrelated?"

"It's possible. And I don't think anyone knew about Jim and me, but the timing is suspicious with Jim's death. If the person was in my office, they likely work there. You know how tight security is."

I glanced at Jake's perplexed face. "The office is on multiple floors and they have their own elevator bank. You need a key card just to get to the elevator bank." I looked back at Eliza. "I mean, it's a big firm. Do you think there was someone else there he had been having an affair with?"

"It's possible. I don't know. It seems like Jim kept a lot of things close to the vest. It would have been a lot of juggling for him. Since we had both agreed to end our marriages, we had been trying to keep our relationship a secret, so when we went public it wouldn't be so seedy. Lately, I had been bringing more work home instead of staying late to avoid being seen with him as much. It's possible Jim had started something with another lawyer, or a paralegal."

Lee was still avoiding me, but she was one of the paralegals at Jim's office. He might have confided in her if he'd gotten stuck in some sort of three-way office romance.

"I have to get going. I'm really sorry, Abby. Hopefully the police will figure out who did this. If you need anything, call. You have my support."

"The police are pretty happy with me as their fall guy. Thank you, Eliza, for telling me this. I don't know if it can help, but it's a start. I'm sorry for your loss."

She smiled wanly. "And I for yours. All right, I have a plane to catch. Text me if you find out anything." She walked off, leaving Jake and I in the office. He had stayed silent throughout the entire exchange.

"What do you think?"

"I think it's more than likely that your husband had not one, but two girlfriends at the office. Or maybe he ditched the first one for Eliza. The girlfriend may not have gotten angry if he said he was going back to his wife, but if she caught him and Eliza together, she could have been really pissed off, even angry enough to kill him."

"Why implicate me? I mean, this is premeditated. She had my coat."

"Right, but it might have just been an inspired choice. That coat is everywhere. It's not like she had to try very hard to set you up."

"Lee worked in Jim's office. Maybe she saw something. I know he talked to her about Eliza, so it's possible she knew about his other affairs."

"You don't think she would have come to you, woman to woman?"

"Ha. Not a chance. She owed all her allegiance to Jim. She has never liked me. Honestly, the past year is the most tolerable our relationship has been, and that's only because I have been so helpful with her son. She was grateful for the extra support. But, no, she would have always kept Jim's secrets. I wonder if she's planning on keeping them to the grave. Maybe if I go over to her place and knock on the door, I can get her to talk to me."

"I can drive you over. It's time I headed over to the shop anyway. There are a few clients coming in today."

"Hopefully Devin is home too." Jake quirked his eyebrow at me questioningly. "He lives across the hall from her, just above the sandwich shop on Southport. I hate to admit this, but I'm a little hurt he didn't show up today."

Jake looked down at his hands, his calloused fingers drumming quickly on the desk before him. "About last night." I looked up in alarm, seemingly in a panic that he might walk back what had been one of the loveliest experiences of my life. "Are we okay? Was it okay? I don't want you to feel pressured into a relationship, and I probably did just that."

"Oh Jake, I came to you last night. I wanted it to happen, as much as you did, and honestly, that is so gratifying. I felt safe waking up in your arms, safe for the first time since Jim's death, as crazy as it sounds." My arms wrapped around his waist. He leaned forward and nuzzled my cheek with his beard.

"I am here for you, always." He leaned toward my

lips and gave me a lingering kiss. The door banged open behind me.

"What the HELL are you doing, Abby?" My brother Will yelled, anger ringing through the small room. The door slammed behind him. "You're in church, for God's sake. Your husband's ashes are twenty feet away waiting for you to take them home and you're in a priest's office making out like a goddamn teenager?" He looked at Jake. "Listen, I don't know who you are, but you need to leave." His chest puffed up in a confrontational stance.

Jake looked from my brother to me. I quickly spoke. "Jake, why don't you wait for me in your car. I'll be out soon, and then we can head back together."

"You're coming back with us, Abby," my brother barked. "Mom has a luncheon planned, remember?"

I blanched, shocked that I had forgotten the day was hardly over yet. My brother was right. I may not owe Jim much, but seeing Jake here had been callous.

"Right. Of course. Jake, I'll text you when I get back to the city. Okay?"

He nodded, giving my elbow a quick squeeze as he walked past my brother. Will had turned imperceptibly to glower at Jake as he passed, then closed the door.

"Do you want to explain yourself?"

"That's Jake, he's my neighbor and he's been so kind during this whole thing. We've been friends for a while, and it just developed into something more."

"Developed when? Were you cheating on Jim?"

"No!" I cried out. "Despite his complete lack of sexual interest in me, personal interest in me, and the fact that I only saw him awake two times a week for the past few years, I was stupidly faithful to him."

"This just started?" Will shook his head disbelieving. "With everything going on right now, you decided this was the time to start a new love affair?"

"Ok, the timing is not ideal. He's just been so nice. It just kind of happened. He told me he's always had a crush on me." Cringing, I realized I sounded like a tween in a Disney rom-com.

"Abby, I know I've been wrapped up in my own life with Carol and the twins the past few years, and maybe I haven't been there for you." He walked toward me, his face softening. "It sucks that you're going through this, but turning to some random guy who has a 'crush' on you the minute your husband is dead? It just seems really heartless and unlike you."

Averting my eyes, I turned away from my brother. "I don't need advice on how to behave, Emily Post. This is my life, and from now on, I am choosing to live it the way I see fit, assuming my choices aren't curtailed by the state putting me in an orange jumpsuit for the next fifty years. We can go back to the house now, and I would prefer it if you kept your opinions on my behavior to yourself."

I stormed out of the office and out the main door. The news cameras were filming, and a small crowd had formed. My father was in the thick of it; a large man was screaming in his face. He turned back to me in anguish. It was Jim's father who stood before him, waving his cane in the air. While not yet old, he'd had an accident on a construction site that had maimed him, causing him to go on disability permanently. Jim had used his father's constant pain as an excuse for not coming to Chicago ever, even for our wedding. The man before me bore a sliver of resemblance to the one in Jim's high school graduation photo, but years of hard living were matted across his features. My father rushed forward to take my arm, and my two brothers gathered round to form a protective barrier.

My father-in-law saw me, unleashing his hatred. "YOU!!! You're the bitch that separated him from me. You took him away from me and then that wasn't enough! You had to kill him too. He used to send me money to help out. You told him he needed to stop, that he didn't need to support his white trash family any more. You think I'm white trash, do you? Well, you're a goddamn murderer!"

My father was pulling me along through the crowd. "Don't say a word," he said quietly in my ear.

Desperate, I struggled to be heard over the crowd. "But I have to tell him I didn't know anything about the money. We kept separate finances. Jim never shared any of that stuff with me."

"Not a word, Abby. The news crews will skewer you, no matter what comes out of your mouth. Just get to the car," Will hissed in my ear.

My mother was behind the wheel of the car. My father shoved me into the backseat and followed me in. "Let's go home, Alice, and please try not to hit anyone. Go as slow as you need to."

My mother's hands shook on the steering wheel. "Yes, John. I understand I'm not supposed to hit anyone." She moved the car slowly, lightly tapping the horn. The police had arrived and started to direct people out of the street. Eventually, we broke free and drove the short distance back to the house. My mother parked the car in the attached garage. She closed the garage door with the overhead buttons and promptly started to cry. My father's strong grip on my arm was starting to hurt. I had not stopped to realize the level of stress they had both been under because of me. They were always so cool and collected. It was hard to believe the chaos of my life had broken them.

"I am so very sorry about everything, Mom."

My mother gave one more large sniffle and nodded. "It's not your fault." Her back straightened. "We will get through this. We will persevere. I have to get ready for the guests now." She quickly exited the car without looking back and I couldn't help feeling I had failed her.

My father still hadn't let go of me. "I'm sorry I can't fix this for you, Abby. You have to forgive your mother. This has all been a great strain."

"Dad, there's nothing to forgive. You guys are allowed to be overwhelmed by the situation. It really sucks. I'm just sorry to have brought all of this unpleasantness to your door. It's invading your privacy and ruining your career. Donors are probably bailing on you left and right."

"That doesn't matter right now. We will find a way out of this and our lives will go back to normal. Don't worry. You need to concern yourself with getting ready for the trial. Your mother and I will be fine." He paused. "When was the last time you heard anything from Jim about his dad?"

I thought back. "Honestly, I don't remember. Jim was always so tightlipped about his family. He didn't like talking about them. I'd had no idea he was sending money home, but, in retrospect, it makes sense. He'd always insisted we keep all of our money separate. We each wrote a check for the mortgage, separate credit cards, I paid the gas, he paid the electric. You know. He'd said it was his pride and we would be equals in everything. He didn't want anyone thinking he'd married me for money. It was bizarre, considering how he valued the connections that came with it. But when it came down to finances, he was very touchy. I guess I'm not answering your question." I looked at my father. "Right before Christmas. I was sending out holiday cards, and offered to send one to his father. Jim told me he would do it himself because his father had recently moved and he couldn't remember the new address off the top of his head. I tried to ask about the reason for the move and Jim immediately changed the subject. Maybe if Jim was no longer supporting him, he had to move into a cheaper place. There was so much going on that I just didn't know about." I buried my face into my father's firm shoulder.

"You'd better pull yourself together. The guests can't be far behind us. Hopefully, no one will stay long."

We went inside. People had started arriving while we were talking in the car. I looked out the window and saw the police cars lined up. How would they decide who was worthy to cross the barrier? Hopefully, Jim's father would not force his way in to make more public accusations, but I suspected that without a news camera's presence, there would be little reason to be so demonstrative. Jim had not talked about his father often, but the few times he had, it was in the nature of guilt. He had not liked his father and had pulled away from him once he left for college. His memories were of a man who had only noticed Jim for his own gain. I remembered one bitter comment from Jim's childhood.

Jim's dad couldn't bother to come to the game, but was more than willing to take the free drinks handed out at the bar to the star point guard's father. The memory of his hurt made me soften toward the memory of my husband. Perhaps my mother was right. Jim had been a complicated man but he had still been my husband. I should take the time to mourn him for my own sake, as well as his. Spending the night with Jake had been wrong. We would have time for our relationship in the future. I made a mental note to text Jake later and tell him that we needed to take a break for a bit.

The next hour was spent wandering between different groups of family and my friends. Though I had seen a few of them at church, none of Jim's friends had come to the house, no doubt questioning my innocence. The crowd began to clear out. My oldest brother said he had to head home—the twins were sick with the flu and Carol had her hands full. He offered to drive me back to Lakeview on his way home.

We mostly drove in silence, occasionally making comments about the food, or bringing up little things the priest had said during the service. As we approached my house, Will reached out to pat my knee. "I'm sorry I came down so hard on you. It just feels like I'm trying to protect you and not doing a very good job. I am well aware that you're an adult who can make her own decisions, and not just my youngest sibling."

"Thanks, I really appreciate that. You're probably right, though. It was in pretty poor taste to make out at the church during my husband's funeral. Like Jerry Springer poor taste." I covered my face, cringing.

"Um, yeah. I think you may have made Jerry Springer seem almost tasteful it was so bad."

I gave his wrist a light slap. "Okay, well thanks for the ride. I hope the kids feel better."

"When's the trial start?"

"A month. It's both a lot of time and not enough."

"Well, I will be there every day to support you, okay?"

"Thanks, big brother. I appreciate you."

Back inside the house, the place was still in a state of disorder after the police. I decided my time would be best spent cleaning. After a few hours of organizing and packing up Jim's things for the donation bin, my spirit began to feel cleansed as well. It was starting to get dark. My stomach growled, reminding me how little I had eaten at my mother's house. I decided the best course of action would be to pick up some soup and head over to Devin's to check on him, hoping his absence today hadn't been in anger. I still wanted to talk to Lee. Maybe Devin could convince her to join us. It was worth a shot.

Chapter 16

I stopped at a deli on Southport, and then continued down the block to Devin's apartment. My phone started to ring. It was Jake. Instead of answering, because my hands were full, I hit ignore. I had not thought through what I would say to him. It would be best if we spoke in person. My phone buzzed with a text.

—*Where are you? We need to talk.*—

I set my bag of soup down on the sidewalk and scooted to the side so I wouldn't block traffic.

—*I'm on my way to see Devin right now. I think we should talk too. Can you stop by later tonight? Maybe around 8?*—

My phone rang again. Jake. Exasperated by his persistence, I hit ignore and shut my phone down.

My brother's words rang in my ear. I knew nothing about Jake. Maybe he was going to prove obsessive if we ever broke up. I shook my head. The past few weeks had only made me start assuming the worst in people. Jake would understand.

Raising my hand up to ring the doorbell, I saw the door was a little stuck and hadn't closed all the way. While sneaking in was duplicitous, it increased the likelihood Devin would actually see me face to face. I walked up the stairs and knocked gently.

"Devin? It's me, Abby. I am sorry you're not feeling well. I brought soup. Can you open up?"

My ear to the door, I heard nothing. Across the hall, the TV was blaring from Lee's place. It was a cozy set up between the two of them, with no other apartments in the building. I gave one last knock on Devin's door and braced myself to confront Lee. Maybe they were together?

"Lee?" I called out, rapping with my knuckles. I heard a shuffle over the TV. "Lee, can you please just talk to me for a minute?"

Through the door, Lee called out, "Go away, Abby. I have nothing to say to you."

"Lee, I just want to talk. I have some questions to ask you. You're obviously upset about Jim's death, but you can't possibly think that I would have pushed him off that platform."

The door opened. "What I think is that this is all your fault! Even if you didn't push him, you drove him into the arms of that other woman. If you could do a passable job of keeping your man happy, none of this ever would have happened."

I stood dumbstruck. Had she guessed that there was another woman in Jim's life or had Jim let her in on the secret?

Looking at Lee, I realized her hair had been unwashed for at least a week. The shadows under her eyes were dark. Her t-shirt was dirty. I had never seen her looking so unkempt. She had prided herself on her looks and dressed to entice the most male attention, embracing her southern belle heritage. She always had on make-up and a curated outfit, no matter what the time of day, even when David had been a newborn.

"I'm so sorry you feel that way, Lee. Can I come in? Jim was likely sleeping with another woman at his office besides Eliza. Maybe he told you about it, or you had some suspicions of your own?"

Rage shimmered beneath Lee's eyes. "What the hell is that supposed to mean? What are you implying?" She spoke loudly, easily heard over the cartoon playing on the television. Behind Lee, David stood in his playpen, chin resting on the edge, watching us.

"There's no implication on my part. I just thought Jim might have spoken with you. You were always so close. My goal is just to clear my name." The TV had been turned on so loud, I was having a hard time concentrating on the conversation. "I'm sorry you didn't feel like you could come to the memorial. I could come in and tell you about it. That might make you feel better, or help you move past your grief?"

"You know nothing about my grief or what I have been through all those long years YOU have been in my life."

My confusion was acute. Clearly, Lee blamed me for something. She had always disliked me, but this was a visceral hatred. I forged on. "Devin didn't come either and he's not home right now. Did you ask him not to go?"

She started to slam the door in my face. Quickly, and with more grace than usual, I managed to shove my boot into the door jamb without toppling over. "Please, Lee, don't shut me out." The sudden movement caused the container of soup to open, sloshing out between us, all over the floor. "I'm sorry. At least let me in so I can clean this up. There's something else spilled on the floor. Is that blood? Did you hurt yourself?"

Lee looked at me wild-eyed at the same time a crash came from the back of the apartment, likely in her bedroom. "What was that?" I started to push past her. This time, she let me in and the door slammed behind me. A muffled cry reached my ears. Opening the door of the primary bedroom, I saw Devin splayed on the bed, his hands trussed above him, tied to the headboard. His ankles were apart, each tied to an opposite leg at the foot of the bed. There was an overturned lamp on the floor. He must have rocked the bed into the nightstand hard enough to knock it over. His mouth strained around his gag, desperate to communicate. I dropped the soup, not caring where it spilled and headed toward him. Too late, I realized he was trying to signal with his eyes to a point behind me. The giant slash across his cheek had stolen my focus. The blood had dripped down his face and neck.

A shooting pain clouded my vision and I crumpled forward, rolling hard to the right as I hit the ground. My evasive maneuver meant Lee's second hit did more damage to my shoulder than my head. She had grabbed a cast iron pan off the stove before following me and was winding up her arm for another attack.

"Lee!!! Please stop!!!" Approaching me, her shoes were slick from the spilled soup. I struggled to get up and past her while she tried to keep her balance. She had dropped the imposing pan in her near fall. Grabbing me by the hair, she pulled me back down, pinning me with her body and started using her fists, banging my head into the floor. I stilled, not quite unconscious, but unwilling to expend any more energy. The pain in my head was blossoming and a wave of nausea overtook me.

As Lee stood up, I rolled over and threw up. In the corner, there was a trash bag full of what was likely clothes, with the merest whisper of a zebra patterned coat sticking out of the top. Lee grabbed my wrists from behind. David was wailing down the hallway. To my ringing ears, it seemed like he was in a tunnel far away. Poor David, all alone with a madwoman.

Lee knelt on my back, looping a cord around my wrists folded behind me. She tied it expertly, as if she were a retired naval officer, and then proceeded to attach the end of the cord to the heavy legs of the armoire to my right. I watched her, my being paralyzed. When she started attaching my ankles to the foot of the bed, consciousness began to break through. I tried to kick at her, my snow boots awkward on my feet.

"Not so high and mighty now, are you? You always acted like such a little spoiled princess. You were entitled to everything. Jim was obsessed with your goddamn pedigree. You were like a show pony to him. He was just using you, though. He never loved you. I was the only woman he ever loved. He thought he'd loved that woman at the office, but she was just a fancier version of you. He would have come back to me."

"So why did you kill him? You could have just waited it out," I said tentatively, trying to keep her focus on me in the thin hope that Devin had loosened his ties when he had knocked the lamp over and would be able to sneak up on her.

She stood up and laughed. "He was trying to say David wasn't his, that he'd deny it left and right. My son! Our son! Our son that was born of the tremendous love we had shared. I couldn't let that happen." She reached back for the pan and gave my knee a quick crack, shattering my patella. I vomited again and blacked out.

When I came to, the room was dark. The clock on the nightstand read a little after eight. The smell of soup, puke, and blood was swirling around the room, a putrid reminder of the day's events. My tongue pressed against the gag in my mouth and I sputtered. Across the hall, a prosaic scene seemed to be playing out. I heard Lee cooing to her young son, willing him to slumber with an old-fashioned lullaby. I was chilled at the way she could mother David while we lay across the hall, bloodied and battered at her hand.

I groaned, trying to shift my swollen leg to a more comfortable position. The pain was excruciating. Tears streaked down my face. "Abby," my brother whispered in the dark. "Are you awake?"

"MMHMHM." I grunted.

Devin spoke again quietly. "I managed to get my gag out, but that's all. I'm going to keep working on my hands. Are you very hurt? Do you think you could wiggle one of your feet against the tie at the bed? I think we are tied up to the same leg?"

I tried to move again. The small effort sent spasms through my body and I cried out through the gag.

"Okay, stop. Oh man, Abby. What are we going to do?" He sighed. "This is all my fault."

We sat quietly in the dark, listening to Lee's singing. My brain was struggling to make sense of his words. How had any of this been his fault? Because he had been dating Lee?

"The other day, you brought up the woman's tattoo. It was a match with Lee's. I realized it was Lee that had been having the affair with Jim. Once you said that, everything fell into place. Their relationship was always so weird. She worshipped him, but she was afraid of him, always afraid of doing the wrong thing. She never wanted to upset him. It always seemed bizarre to care so much about what your cousin thought, but it made a lot more sense if she was in love with him. I came back here to confront her. It didn't occur to me that she murdered him. I was just mad she was playing me for a fool, using me to make him jealous. That kid is the spitting image of Jim. Seriously, Abby, how did you not realize that the kid was Jim's?"

I grimaced, my mind whirring through the pain. My brother's usual gruffness was welcome this time. He was right—we'd all been so blind, just because they had said they were cousins. I thought back to the first time I had met Lee back in college, coming out of his bedroom, guilt etched on their faces. I had never questioned the nature of their relationship, always willing to take Jim's words at face value. The affair had been going on for years. It had likely started when they were teenagers. I wondered if they actually were cousins. That would at least explain why their romance had to be kept secret. Jim had been so proud of David, of his son. He had pinned our fertility issues on me because of this living proof of his ability to sire children.

"Anyway, she slipped up. She thought I was accusing her of killing Jim. I had only thought to accuse her of cheating on me. She came at me with a knife and took a slash at my face. While I was fighting her off, David came running over and toppled into me. I went to grab him and try to get him out of the way. That's when she grabbed that ridiculous pan and knocked me out. When I came to, I was here on the bed."

His voice cracked and I realized he was struggling to talk. His mouth must be parched. Who knew when she'd last given him water? I felt awful knowing that I had been two blocks away at Jake's place while all this was happening. Thinking about Jake reminded me that my phone was off. Even if anyone started to think about my disappearance, it would be hard to track my location. I had disappeared somewhere on Southport. Devin's phone would be pinging from the building he lived in. It was hardly suspicious. I wondered how long we had. She had to kill us. The sandwich shop closed at eight. I knew from experience, often stopping by after work for my frequent solo dinners. The building would soon be quiet once the employees downstairs had cleaned up for the night.

Devin seemed to be echoing my thoughts. "She's going to have to kill us. Or skip town and leave us here, knowing we will starve to death before anyone finds us.

"I know, I know, lack of water would kill us first. I can hear you thinking at me, Abby. You're always such a know it all."

I tried to smile through the gag, grateful for my brother's half-hearted attempt at lightening the mood. If she did kill us, it would mean dragging the bodies down the steps to her car and then dropping us somewhere. She could easily move my dead body, but Devin was a large man. He would be unwieldy. The jacket peeking out of the bag made me think she wasn't being rational. Holding on to the coat was tantamount to a confession. She'd probably been holed up here in this apartment, playing over Jim's death again and again. When Devin had stopped by, her instinct was to assume he was there to accuse her of murder. Devin was right. Lee's obsession with Jim had taken over her life. She would be devastated at his loss, even if it had been at her hand.

The night of the Christmas dinner came back to me. That had been when things had shifted between them. Perhaps Jim had broken it off with her that night, assuming she wouldn't make a scene in front of my family?

David was still crying in the other room. We could hear her trying to settle him. Time was running out. If she was going to kill us, it would be in the next few hours. I struggled to wriggle my wrists out of their bindings. My brother's movements were slow above me, his motions small and precise, trying to keep the sound to a minimum not to call her attention back to us. The pain in my leg was so intense that I had little strength left. Lee's bedroom was at the back of the apartment, overlooking the alley. The workers' voices from downstairs filtered up through the window as they tossed the trash into the garbage, signaling the end of their shift. Panic coursed through me. I had anchored on to their presence in my mind like a life raft. I looked at the clock. It was a few minutes after nine.

Making little progress, I made a small noise to get my brother's attention. "I hear you," he whispered. "One of my wrists is almost free. I wish she'd left the lights on in here."

We both stilled as a loud knock echoed through the apartment from the front door. Had one of our brothers thought to find us here? Lee could be heard walking out of David's room across the hall. "Who's there?"

"It's Fedex, ma'am. Sorry, it's so late. You're my last stop, but you have to sign for it. Do you mind opening up?" yelled the muffled voice.

My senses began to tingle. I mentally willed Devin to start yelling for help. He echoed my thoughts. "I'll start screaming after we hear the door open. Hopefully, the guy will rush in, or think to run and call the cops."

The muffled voice was loud and insistent. "Ma'am? The package is for Lee Simon. Is that you, ma'am?"

"Yes, it's me. I'm coming." We heard the door click open. Suddenly, there was a yell.

"You!" She screeched. There were shoving noises and a clatter of something knocked over. "Get out of here!"

"I just want to talk to you. Where's Abby?" The voice belonged to Jake. My heart leapt. How had he found me?

"In here!!!" Devin shouted. "Be careful!" My brother warned. "She has us tied up!" There was more banging, and I heard the sound of a body being slammed into a wall. Heavy male footsteps came down the hall. The door was splintered as Jake kicked it open.

"Abby, are you okay?"

Jake stood in the doorway. He had his arms wrapped around Lee, her wrist bent awkwardly behind her back.

"Put her in the closet. There's a chair right there you can prop against it."

Jake used his foot to scoot the chair closer to the closet. Lee was struggling against him. I watched him try to be gingerly with her, knowing he wouldn't want to hurt a woman. She managed to reach down and bite his hand. His grasp tightened on her wrist and twisted. Her cries of pain caused David's wails to begin again in earnest across the hallway. Jake then rammed her into the wall next to the closet door. Caught off-guard, she briefly stopped struggling. Jake took the opportunity to shove her into the closet, slamming the door and swiftly bracing it with the propped chair.

Quickly looking between us, Jake pulled out the hunting knife that he always carried and bent down. "Abby, don't move. I'm going to get you free in a second." He cut through the cord and freed my wrists and my feet. He turned quickly and did the same for Devin. I tried to lift my numb arms to my face to pull my gag down. Jake was back at my side. "Here. I got it." Gently he looped his finger under the coarse cloth and tugged it down.

"Abby." His voice was tender and I started to cry. He pulled me close with loose arms, unsure of my injuries. I felt him feather kisses into my hair, seemingly unaware of the vomit laced through it. "Thank goodness you're okay."

Devin was next to the bed, attempting to stand. He was too weak and fell back. "Water. Can you bring me some water?"

Jake looked at the closet, checking it again on his way to the kitchen, and came back with two bottles of water from the fridge. He handed one to Devin and held the other to my lips. "I'm going to call 911 and get you an ambulance, Abby?"

I nodded. "Devin too. I think he probably had a concussion."

"You're going to have a hell of a scar, too, man."

"I heard chicks dig scars," my brother attempted to smile, the pain of moving his face turning it into a grimace.

"How on earth did you know to come here?"

Jake paused, his phone in his hand. "You told me to come over to your place at eight but then you weren't home. I was worried you were going to try to end things. You'd hung up without talking to me earlier. And then you never responded to my texts. I sat on your back porch waiting until about eight thirty, then I got pissed off thinking you had stood me up. I walked over to the corner bar to get a drink. Nicole was there. She told me she had seen the woman that had been with Jim at the bar walking around the neighborhood and managed to take a picture with her phone. I recognized Lee. You had introduced us a couple of months ago after the Cubs game. I didn't know what it meant. I tried calling you again but your phone was off. I remembered you had told me she lived in this building, opposite Devin, so I came over."

"Why did you say you were the FedEx guy?"

"I thought I had a better chance of talking to her if she opened the door. I didn't really know that she would open it if I said I was the possible boyfriend of her dead lover's almost ex-wife. Lying seemed the more straightforward route." He stepped away to call 911. I felt myself about to pass out again.

"I got you," Devin said, pulling himself down to the floor next to me. "You're safe. We'll take care of you."

Chapter 17

When I woke again, it was in the sterile room of a hospital. My mother's worried face leaned in, grasping my hand. I had been heavily sedated. The weight of the cast felt heavy around my knee.

"Abigail?"

"Hi, Mom."

"Abigail, thank goodness you're ok. We were so worried about both of you. Devin has been released. They put him on fluids for a while but he's going to be ok."

"Did they sew him up?" I asked, my speech slurred.

"Yes, I called Margaret's husband. He's one of the top plastic surgeons in the city and he came straight down to do it, but it's going to be a terrible scar. Are you hungry, do you want some juice?" She reached for the Styrofoam cup on the rolling tray by my bed. I shook my head.

"Lee?" I asked, hoping she hadn't escaped while I had taken my drug induced hiatus from the living.

"She's in jail, awaiting a psych evaluation. Poor little David's with DCFS. I wanted to take him home with us but they said we weren't any relation. Lee's mother is on her way up from Tennessee to take him home with her."

I tried to form Jake's name on my lips. My mother

shook her head. "You're still very groggy, dear. Don't worry about a thing. Everything is fine. They've dropped the charges against you and you're safe. We'll talk about it after you rest a while more."

I found my eyes struggling to stay open. I let myself drift away.

Waking again later, I felt more lucid. Devin and Jake were in the room this time, sitting next to each other. They were taking turns playing a video game, seemingly bonded for life after the traumatic experience, as only men can bond. The air was comfortable between them and I smiled.

"I'm on my deathbed, and you guys are playing video games?"

Devin smiled, his face half covered by bandages. "About time you woke up. It's been three days. They kicked me out of the hospital yesterday. I always said Mom and Dad coddled you too much."

"I'd throw my pillow at you but there's no way I'd be able to get out of bed and get it back."

Jake took my hand and kissed it. "Hey you. It's nice to see those blue eyes of yours again."

My heart thumped at his sweet words. Here was the man who had stood by me during the worst days of my life. He had risked his own life to save me. "I love you too." My voice was soft, barely above a whisper.

Jake's smile spread across his face. "All it took was rescuing you from a psychopath to get you to fall in love with me?"

"Nope, that's what it took to make me realize I was in love with you."

"You two lovebirds are making me sick. I'm going to go find Dad and tell him you're awake. He's been dealing with the media frenzy all day. This is going to give him a sure win next time he runs, though. He's eating it up." Devin stood. "I'm glad you're okay, little sis." He walked out the door.

I turned to Jake. "Maybe I should have saved that little comment for when it was just the two of us. Devin has got to be hurt over Lee's betrayal. I think he had real feelings for her."

"Yeah, it's hard finding out your girlfriend is a murderer. I only date girls accused of murder. Not ones that blatantly admit to killing people."

"Did Lee confess?"

"Yeah, Mikey came by while you were sleeping and sat us all down. Your parents are really nice, by the way, though this wasn't quite how I imagined getting to know your family."

"I'm glad you like them, but can you please fill me in on what actually happened?"

"Apparently, your charming husband had broken up with Lee right before he broke up with you. He'd been financially supporting her for years, and the stipend had become more generous when their son was born. He didn't allow her to put his name on the birth certificate, though. His plan after divorcing you was to waltz out of their lives, cutting them off financially, and denying paternity."

"Why? Why not end the relationship but still provide for his own son?"

"Apparently Eliza's father was suspicious of him. Jim was worried he would investigate Jim's finances in an attempt to make sure Jim wasn't going after Eliza just for the money, although she has so damn much of it, I don't know what difference it would make. Rich people are so weird about money."

"Why didn't she just tell Eliza? She could have had a DNA test done easily. That would have been a sure way to blow up their relationship."

"While Jim was no longer supporting her, he had left everything to little David in case of his demise, to be split later if there were other kids that came along. If Lee were to approach Eliza with the truth of David's paternity, Jim threatened to cut him out of the will. Lee was left out completely. She thought by killing him, she would have control over the money, but he had set up the trust in such a way she can't access it at all. That wasn't clear until after the will was read."

"Wow. Poor Lee. Were they even cousins?"

"Yes, apparently that's why the relationship was always so secretive. Lee's mother is Jim's aunt on his mom's side. Jim's mom had always been a wild child. First drinking and then drugs, which ended up with her overdosing when Jim was little. Jim's dad wasn't much of a parent so Lee's mom stepped in with his upbringing. She raised Jim and Lee as siblings. When puberty hit, she suspected there might be something going on between the two of them, but they always denied it.

"After they had both left for college, Lee's mom found some steamy letters they had written to each other and went ballistic. It was years before she spoke to either of them. Lee didn't care. She just wanted to be with Jim. He was rattled by his aunt's reaction, knowing marrying your cousin was considered trashy, even illegal in some places, and that it wouldn't fit with his plans for a successful legal career but he couldn't stay away from Lee. He convinced her to keep their relationship a secret, promising that one day they would get to be together, once he was successful enough to weather any scandal. According to Lee, your marriage to him was always supposed to be temporary. Jim had told her that your family would fast track his career with their connections. Why she believed all this nonsense is beyond me, but she loved him with all her heart and it blinded her."

I shook my head. "It blinded me too. I can't believe Jim kept all this stuff from me for years. He'd told me a bit about his dad but wouldn't really elaborate ever. The story he told about his mother was a blatant lie. I feel like such a fool."

"You're a kind and honest person, Abby, which means you always believe the best in people. I love that about you." He kissed me. I shifted to embrace him, the movement causing a shooting pain through my leg.

"AAAHHHH!"

"Ah, yes, your leg. This has really put a damper on my plans."

"I'm so sorry my knee has been smashed to a pulp. What plans would those be?"

"You don't remember?" He wiggled his eyebrows suggestively.

"Sorry, it's been a long week. Can I get a little hint?"

"We were supposed to be jetting off to Hawaii for our super romantic month-long date."

"Right. I think that might be too long a flight for me right now."

He shook his head, feigning disappointment. "I guess Hawaii will have to wait. I do have another idea, though. I have a little cottage in Indiana. No stairs, right on Lake Michigan. Why don't you let me take you there? I'll help you recuperate. We'll read and roast marshmallows and make love in front of the fireplace." He took my hand, gently kissing the inside of my palm.

A shiver passed through me. "Somehow, you've made Indiana more appealing than Hawaii. I didn't know that was possible."

"Is that a 'yes'?" He smiled.

"Yes, definitely a yes." My still naïve and trusting heart soared.

A word about the author...

M. J. Slater is a native Chicagoan. After attending the University of Chicago, she spent 15 years in finance. She loves film noir, yoga, and walking along Lake Michigan with her dog. She lives in the suburbs with her husband and two girls. This is her first novel.
www.mjslaterauthor.com